The Quest

By

Giorgio Kostantinos

authorHOUSE
1663 Liberty Drive, Suite 200
Bloomington, Indiana 47403
(800) 839-8640
www.authorhouse.com

This book is a work of fiction. Places, events, and situations in this story are purely fictional and any resemblance to actual persons, living or dead, is coincidental.

First published by AuthorHouse 10/22/04

ISBN: 1-4184-7474-6 (sc)
ISBN: 1-4184-6942-4 (dj)

Library of Congress Control Number:2004098552

Printed in the United States of America
Bloomington, Indiana

This book is printed on acid-free paper.

The Quest

A special dedication goes to my family, without their support I fear to think of how diffrent my life would be. Out of all the things in life it has been the unconditional love they have for me that has proven to be the most important. My life is everything because of it, and would have been nothing without it.

Their continue support, even when I appear to be at my lowest, has been the greatest gift God could have given me. It is they who have shaped my life and because of this, I have been able to grow into the person I am today. So a special dedication goes out to them, they are the reason I have been able to achieve my goals, and with the publication of this book, I believe they have achieved theirs.

I may not say it enough, but I love you.

--Gus! :)-

Dedication

This book is credited to a woman I once cared for, and her I, but I made some mistakes.

I did apologize, but I feel as if I should go into details. Friendships can only go two ways, they rarely last forever. One is to grow closer and more intimate, but she herself felt against it. A bit of an age difference, five years, go figure.

The other is to grow apart, goals change and interest fades. It is an unpleasant fact of life. Eventually our friendship would have ended, but the way it happened. She is a beautiful woman who wanted nothing more than success; she has intelligence consideration, and devotion. A kind and caring woman who I put in an ugly situation, she didn't deserve that. That is why I apologize, for what she was expected to endure. All things come to an end, my apology was not meant to rekindle some lost spark, I can't fix that. I will always care for her and her son, and always wish them the best of luck. I feel confident that one day she will find her calling, if she hasn't already. I don't know, I don't talk to her much any more. In my life, I need to lose something important in order to move forward.

This book is dedicated to her; I don't believe I would have written it, if not for the foolish mistakes I made. So for that I thank them, and forever wish them the best.

L.J.B. and S.B.

Gk.

The Quest

You are about to embark on a journey, some real, some not, it's yours to decide.

But you are about to find out how far a human endeavor can take one.

A tale of love, spoiled by hates.

A quest for such unimaginable power, it would shatter even the finest mind.

Where the word impossible holds no meaning.

A quest beyond the reach of any.

Where a man driven by love, will find out in the end, if it was all worth it.

Let the journey begin

Written by: Giorgio Kostantinos

Table of Contents

Prologue

Conscious thoughts can take one only so far, there are times the subconscious must be keyed into something greater than itself.

Somewhere within the deep wells of the mind.

Within this vortex lies universal knowledge unimaginable, within this realm thought encounters no barriers.

Only then, are all things possible.

As I stand alone in my emptied apartment I'm engulfed with thought.

Thinking about what once was but is no longer, errors, miscalculations, mistakes on my part.

Vanity was once my corner stone, an ego so large even my broad shoulders fell weak.

I turn to find myself no longer alone.

Josh, a one-time business associate and friend speaks.

Gk, I just heard your misfortunes, but you made some promises and she wished to know why you were not laboring at the tasks ahead of you.

Your words were bold but your actions didn't reflect them as such. So why weren't you out bringing this boon to them?

Gazing out my window, I answer his question.

Because, I gazed into the depths of wisdom.

Such knowledge was required to properly accomplish my goals, one only realizes such truths when he has been beyond the vail and returned.

Josh looks bewildered, I don't think he was prepared for the answer I replied, but in his words he hinted that she had felt used, betrayed, and lied to.

Josh has no reply, so I continue.

Need I remind you, that even when we first met, her well-being was my only concern!

No other has ever, ever cared for her as so.

Josh replies, you'll have to prove, with your newly acquired knowledge that you have learned from your mistakes. Or is all this merely a ploy Proud Gk cooks up for his own personal amusement?

His words are harsh but direct, he is not the first to question my motives, but the heart is far more mysterious than the mind, and later even my heart will hold no secrets. I reply to his comments.

My love for her drove me to shoulder the awesome tasks set before me and I tackled them with unbridled enthusiasm, but don't forget the man you address. For Gk is not one to stand united with a single woman, my heart is not an easy item to acquire. I've been down that road before and vowed never to suffer through it again.

Josh questions, and you think this is fair to women?

Most definitely, but certain women seem to escape that vow and I find myself caring, she was one of those women.

Because of her, I sought to refine and increase my talents in order to become a better man.

Josh asks for clarification.

I set forth goals through which to focus my awesome might.

Goals? Josh questions.

Didn't you not once achieve your desires only to destroy the engagement by your one time love?

Yes! Working toward my goals I failed to realize, but at that time I did not perceive the true nature of love.

Fortunately, my time back home has opened my eyes.

With love, no obstacle would be too great.

It's unfortunate that most people take the simplest things for granted; they have no notion of the true nature of life's most simplest of treasures.

They take them as crude notions or worse, they are ungrateful.

You are forever the wiser and best suited, aren't you Gk? Josh says in a sarcastic manner.

All and always, to accomplish my dreams I reply.

So Josh, do you see why I seek out a possibly speedier solution to the problem set me?

Might I add, that the first goal I wish to complete will have me working back on the drive.

Josh smirks and replies, you do remember the scornful resentment she has for you?

The mistakes you made are not easily forgiven; some people might enjoy seeing you suffer the losses you have.

I'm well aware of that; my face grows sourer as the truth is not always an easy pill to swallow.

And though she will always have a place in my heart and I wish her the best, the light now burns dim and my goals are now for my own personal accomplishment.

I assure you, it is merely coincidental.

Our journey once crossed paths, but I now start anew.

You are a changed man Gk, I wish you luck.

My luck will hold, my quest begins.

Goals of such unimaginable difficulties, once they are completed . . .

Redemption

I was once in-charge of a successful company, but during an extended vacation I was voted out.

A rule I had placed to prevent incompetence, it would prove to be my downfall.

My dismissal had nothing to do with my vacation rather several weeks prior, I would work only several hours a week and leave neglecting my responsibilities. I don't blame their decision, it was one of the many mistakes I made.

I enter a local establishment and order a drink.

An old friend had told me that Joe had recently acquired a location on the drive, he apparently transgressed boundaries set by his old broker.

His location is under a mile from the woman I once cared about, could the fates be anymore cruel?

Working there is not something I would have dared in past times, but that has all changed.

Now I am free of outside interference, my desires have changed, my priorities differ, I no longer pollute my body. Now, I fear nothing, except failure! My trek takes me to different locations, it feels as if I'm experiencing deja vu' an inconceivable notion.

I'm consistently meeting different people during this trek, some know her and they each exert their own influences.

A spiritually and physically taxing experience, for a lesser man this would prove to be a wasted endeavor, but I endure as always.

People; like all outside influences, have a minimal effect on me. I always hold true to myself, for I am Gk, a unique individual during any era.

My journey ends dramatically, how else would one enter the hectic arena known as the Drive?

From here springs all that is, it is the fulcrum of tourism. Of course, Joe's location rests at the entrance and there are people.

They are people of mixed standings, the perfect sentries. They sense me immediately, but they were pitched and toured by a less formidable broker than myself. They surround me and ask questions, but I have no time or desire to answer, so I get rid of them. Joe sits at his location, and I approach.

Greetings Joe.

Proud Gk, what's going on? I thought you gone.

No longer, I reply.

What brings you to such a hectic location? Joe questions.

You do! I've come to help build your new location.

Your intent I applaud Gk, but your motives I question. Great Gk is not known for his generosity.

But my pragmatism is legendary, I reply.

Joe asks for a further explanation.

I have just returned and suffered heavy losses, I was one of the best brokers at one time, but mistakes were made. I need to start over, and rebuilding is not going to be easy.

With a blank expression on his face Joe replies, not without first finding a new partner.

Exactly, someone capable of working well in this business.

And you figured helping me Gk would earn you my undying gratitude?

Definitely Joe, with the emphasis on the undying part of gratitude.

I stand there looking at Gk and I say nothing, but does this fool actually think I need a partner such as himself, money is my only want.

Perhaps I should play along with this dolt, I'll never be successful on my own. Gk's abilities are nothing when compared to mine, once he helps me I shall deal with him accordingly.

But tell me Gk, do you think this location needs two people?

No, but with another location the two of us should be able to reclaim our success. You work at this location Joe and sell tickets, while I work at my location and purchase tickets.

It seems as sound a plan as any, I'll contact my backers and we'll get you a location on Monday.

In the meantime, I work with Joe at his location.

Even with the two of us, I can sense the capabilities this location has.

Monday rolls around and I begin working my location.

Joe is doing well and I do my best to match him, it's been awhile, but this business is simple.

Several weeks go by and it seems as if this partnership is a success, I buy all the tickets and Joe turns around and sells them. We are getting recognized as formidable brokers, several locations close do to our success. I go visit Joe at his location.

With excitement Joe stands up and says, at long last I'm back. In truth, I had given up all hope.

I reply and tell him that within Gk's heart hope always springs eternal.

Joe asks, how can I properly express my gratitude for your valiant efforts?

Without giving me a chance to reply, Joe continues.

How can I properly thank one who has betrayed his woman in order to help me?

With sarcasm Joe asks, moreover, how could I ever trust one such as you?

I smirk, and a confused look appears on Joe's face.

With force, I backhand Joe across the face and a three-inch gash opens above his left eye.

As he falls to the ground, I reply to his comments.

Conceited fool! Do you really think I would abandon my desires to work with one such as you?

I reach down and remove a small device from Joe's person. In truth, the only reason I helped you was for this.

Joe begins to stand and asks, how?

You want an explanation, I'll give you one.

This is the nexus of tourism, a crossroad where locals and tourists bond. At this location, there are no dichotomies your pathetic pitches need in order to work.

Joe states that they have been working for him so far, before he can continue I interrupt.

That's because your bosses are kind, they allow you that luxury so your location will be more tolerable, but I doubt they'll indulge you ever again.

You see Joe, that is why they placed you here at the entrance to the Drive, even they weren't sure you couldn't acquire any tickets.

With my back turned, I face the street and continue.

Of course, they had no idea that I would come to your aid, and they wouldn't have been able to stop me. You see Joe, I am one of those people who are outside tourism's usual realm of influences.

Your bosses have no authority over me, so they can't stop my comings and goings.

Unfortunately for you, they have been alerted to your practices and are on their way now, so I must be going. My guess, that your next location will probably be nowhere as comfortable, for that I apologize. I get in my car and begin to pull away when Joe's bosses show up.

They seem quite upset with him, and he tries to tell them that it's not his fault.

Joe tries to blame me, but to no avail.

Just then, Joe's bosses begin to raise their voices and at the same time I turn the corner and they are no longer in view.

My first objective completed!

This was once the property of my one time ally John Walker, but he was a fool.

He had no idea what wonders this tool could accomplish.

With it, any living being can be located, no secrets can hide, never before has such information been available.

I return home and within moments, Josh appears and asks me if I'm truly over her?

What? Out of all the questions that could be asked, that was the least I would have expected.

Josh expresses that she is waiting for an answer, so I do not disappoint.

Surely she can recognize a coincidence when she sees one, how can she ask such a question of me?

How many times must I apologize for the mistakes I have made? Even tough I cared deeply for her, we were friends at best, nothing more.

I swore to her I have changed and there will be no interference on my part.

And despite the mistakes I've made in the past, you know when Gk's word is given, it is always honored.

Josh stands there for a second or two and replies, that she accepts this testament and wishes me good fortune on my quest.

Josh turns to leave and once again I am alone with my thoughts.

Thinking about how she is keeping an eye on me, but that is what I expected.

Which means I must be doubly careful, I don't want her to think that the only reason I'm on the Drive is for her.

I care enough about her to stay away, and when the moment is right I will divulge my plans to her.

However, right now it is best not to even consider the dire ramifications of such a premature discloser.

A popular franchise, and a popular hangout for locals and tourists alike. It is a strategic location to utilize that fact, but as of late it has been consistently empty. So they have been forced to invent and reinvent themselves, it is the perfect location for the guy who currently has possession of my second goal. Where else can this guy regularly test his broker skills? Daily dealing with one tourist and waiting for another, always letting his employees think that he's the best in the business.

For a guy who lives to cheat people, this business is perfect. Of course, when you hire people away from the carnival, it's not hard to tell them the check is in the mail. Their mental capacity is limited, and it's not difficult to deceive them. Who would question him? Until someone stands up he'll continue to cheat them, and why not? If they allow it to happen they're getting exactly what they deserve, but his location is limited due to the lack of tourists in the area. So it's only a matter of time before he is forced to close the doors, he has no idea of how the tourist trade works. He actually thinks he is the best in the business and credits his survival to his tourism prowess, it shall prove his undoing. I arrive at my destination and watch as he speaks to a family, soon I will have back that which is rightfully mine. I call him out and state that when he's finished with those children, I would have word's with him.

He turns and faces me, with a blank expression on his face he asks, Proud Gk, what do you want?

My reply is simple; I've come to take back what is mine.

He begins to walk toward me and asks, what needs have you of it?

None! A rematch is all I really want, will I find it here?

He begins to laugh, yes! But you will also find defeat here.

For I will take your challenge, I cannot be beat.

His friends stand by encouraging him, they will soon bear witness to his downfall.

He is now in front of me, he takes a step back and launches a huge right, he misses as I circle around him.

I grab him by the back of his shirt and comment that he telegraphs his punches years ahead of there coming, as I turn him around he yells, what?!

Never mind, and I unleash a massive right-hook to his jaw.

It backs him up and he tries to regain his footing.

You dare mock me Gk, for that you will pay!

I doubt it, and now he begins to charge.

I move out of the way and he pitches forward, off balance hitting the floor hard.

I must say you are turning out to be a great disappointment to me, I really expected more of a challenge from you. Can you here me while laying flat on your face?

He stands up and dusts himself off; you can see that he is no match, he is barely able to speak.

You certainly are a tricky one Gk, from this point on I will take it slow and easy with you.

I stand at guard with my arms raised and reply to his comments, you obviously misunderstood the point of this encounter.

I throw another right hand, catching him across the ear and he goes down for a second time.

There is not going to be anything easy about it!

He is slower getting up this time, his face is bloodied and he replies, it will take more than that to beat me Gk.

I get back in a fighting stance, perhaps.

I throw a quick left, then again perhaps not.

He blocks my punch and replies, there are no perhaps about it.

You can feel the anger coming from this guy, the deranged man speaks.

Once I put my mind to something, I am unstoppable.

He starts to walk toward me, he continues to speak and with his anger I can barely understand him.

Nobody in town can curb my righteous anger, nobody can stand against me.

No one is capable of surviving my right hand, he's right on me and continues to mutter.

I am unbeatable, and I. . .I. . .then unexpectedly he trips and pitches forward.

You talk too much; I catch him under the chin splitting his jaw, and you think too little.

He gets up quickly, the bloodied man so enraged he yells, such tricks and taunts shall avail you not in this rematch Gk! As you are about to learn to your sorrow! We lock hands in much like a test of strength, and you can see that neither of us is going to give in.

His friends yell encouragement, come on, you can beat Gk!

The expression of rage on his face grows as he asks, so you think you can win this contest?

I've encountered people twice your ability and have always overcome them.

He releases his grip, steps back and swings.

I move, but the energy exerted in his punches is almost inconceivable.

I already begin to see him slow, blood drips from his mouth as he speaks. His friends have come to his aid trying to hold him back, but to no avail.

He throws an uppercut and misses, it seems his strength grows in direct proportion to his anger.

In many ways I assume this is what it would be like fighting a drug-induced madman, a conflict I sought to avoid over the years.

He throws a massive right hand and it nearly hits its mark, my chin.

I am able to move in time, and he now does the unexpected, he quits swinging.

He backs off when he nearly had me, this madman has gone insane as he yells, damnation!

Gk you are no fighter, a true fighter doesn't duck and block, but it won't win the day for you.

Anger has totally consumed this madman; the look on his face is pure rage.

His friends try to hold him back as the blood is wiped from his face, but he won't listen and I only came here for one reason.

You gotta stop! Gk has content in his eyes, and he might . . .

He pushes through his friends, I cannot be beat!

The madman yells.

I am the better fighter, you'll never beat me Gk!

Then, if programmed, he makes the move I have been waiting for.

He backs up toward the end of the street, these madman types are all so predictable.

They jump themselves into a righteous steroid frenzy, thinking fighting is the answer to all problems.

They actually think their fists can gain for them what their puny intellects cannot.

It is much like dealing with a child, an over-sized child, but a child nonetheless.

And this infantile beerier is truly insane, but it will benefit him little.

In the end, the mind always proves to be the most powerful muscle.

He is almost on me, charging like a bull and his friends have become spectators to this contest. With some closing their eye's as they already sense the outcome.

He's nearly on me, at the last second, much like a matador, I move.

He goes crashing through a window, glass shatters everywhere and his location becomes the only victim of his anger.

The reaction continues along the side, and in turn pushes him into his location and it is devastated.

Of course, he had no idea that I would move, but I did.

I also knew that his unchecked anger could be manipulated to use against him.

There's a brief silence and then you here, I won.

No one can stand against me, he says. I won it all!

I approach the bloodied madman, shattered glass is everywhere and his location is in ruins.

He seems to be bleeding from every conceivable spot, he is truly hurt.

I ask him, have you won?

It looks to me that all you've managed to do is destroy the location you fought for, and left yourself unemployed.

A bewildered madman looks around at the damage he's caused and replies, I'll battle you for your location.

And why should I agree to such a contest?

He answers, for the honor of combat.

Rubbish, I don't feel like fighting.

Then Gk, you are a wimp.

It looks to me that you're the only one hurt, you begin to bore me, farewell.

He yells, wait, wait! You can't leave me here like this!

I turn and smile because the deal I have been waiting for is ready to be struck.

I answer him, why not? You'll heal from your wounds, but I imagine the owners of this location will want compensation for the damage you've caused.

His girlfriend comes up to me, please, I beg you, take him to a hospital.

My reply, I will for a price.

What price?

I want back what rightfully belongs to me!

A confused look appears on his face, what?

Forget it, sooner or later someone will come by and help me.

I reply, that they'll probably remember what kind of monster you are and leave you.

His confused expression yields, he realizes my point. Fine take it, it never worked out for me anyways. You will still take me even though it didn't work?

Gk always honors an agreement, hop in the back and I'll take you.

He gets in and I take him to the closest hospital, I believe this hospital will be suitable?

He replies, yes. I know this hospital well, I should have no problems . . .hey . . .hey, what are you doing?

Dropping you off at the closest hospital, and I did.

Our agreement never stipulated anything about front door service, now get out.

I wonder if he'll survive this encounter, he should.

Perhaps I should have treated him better, after all he did provide me with a great deal of amusement and helped me accomplish my second goal.

Now two are complete, my third takes me south.

Chris Walters, once his only concern was creating floral beauty. This desire led him to track down a formula to use as a tool for this end, but it also put him in contact with my associates and awakened a hunger for power within him.

Perhaps this drive has been quieted, because as of late he has broken off his associations with them and returned to merely tending his gardens.

That is exactly where I find him, and a truly magnificent garden it is.

Those are strange words coming from you Gk.

Let me assure you Chris, that despite my past mistakes, I can still appreciate beauty, as well as respect those who create it.

Would you care to join me on my rounds Gk?

It would be a pleasure.

As we walk through his gardens, I'm at awe from
the wonders I see.

Flowers of every conceivable size and color, all in bloom. There are roses which bloom as large as my head, there are birds flying about.

A canopy of trees, pathways leading in all directions with each one revealing its own treasure.

This surely must be one of the most beautiful places on Earth.

We walk down a path and I've been wondering Chris, why you no longer run with your associates?

I've no need too, he replies.

Their goal was always the acquisition of power and yet more power, all I truly ever craved was the peace of my gardens.

Then why did you ever take up with that crowd in the first place?

Much like a professor stands to lecture, Walters explains. We shared one common objective, scientific formulas. I possessed one years ago and my gardens never bloomed so magnificently.

I was determined to regain this prize, even if it meant dealing with the likes of them.

Now that I have, my gardens surely must be the most beautiful in the entire world.

Behold, my attention is directed to a bush of what appears to be golden roses.

His statement I cannot argue with.

We enter a courtyard, shall we sit and enjoy the greens for a while Gk?

An excellent idea Chris.

We sit directly across from each other on concrete benches covered in moss with willow trees all around us and vines cluttering the floor around our feet.

Our conversation continues, of course you do know why I'm here Chris?

You want my formula.

I need it to further my own dreams.

And your dreams are more important than my gardens?

I sit with my arms at either side, take a deep sigh and explain. Yes! My goals must override all others, my dreams and desires cannot be denied.

You realize Gk, I cannot give up that formula without a fight.

My voice grows firm, I wish you'd reconsider that decision Chris. Surely you must realize that your skills are nothing compared to mine.

In an equally firm tone, Chris responds.

Yes Gk, and I also know you have already completed two of your goals, which makes you a truly unbeatable opponent. However, I too must be true to my desires and needs.

I have no wish to hurt you Chris.

Nor I you Gk, but our dreams are at odds.

At that moment, when he uttered those words, I knew the mistake I have made.

I fell for Chris's trap, he pulls a lever off to his side. Ropes engulf my body and within moments I feel like a living mummy. Only my eye's are revealed, I can feel the life being squeezed from my being.

But I am Gk, and such trickery will not best me.

I stand, arms fully extend I break free and dust myself off.

Poor Chris, you truly have no idea what that formula does. That formula comes from before recorded times, and I believe it might even be the cornerstone to the scientific community.

With them combined, all facets of actually can be controlled, I take a moment and explain.

Walker's is the key to all information of every living being.

The one I acquired during my rematch, backs all others, it is the foundation of the dynasty I now envision.

And with your formula, I possess the gift of time.

With victory at hand I explain to my old friend his mistakes.

You didn't consciously realize that was your formula's secret property.

With it, the streams of time can be reconstructed as easily as a child builds a sandcastle.

Only your subconscious barely perceived this formula's potential; I take one last look at his gardens and sadly continue.

That is how you created your wondrous gardens.

Your plants grew so rapidly because you raced them through their growth cycles, and they bloomed eternally because you froze them the moment they reached the zenith of their beauty.

Botanical splendor, never before achieved.

I stand before the golden roses, unfortunately without the formulas aid the gardens beauty won't last, and watch as they crumble.

For that I am truly sorry and I hope that you'll understand my regrets, even though you can no longer hear my words.

I turn, my old friend has had the life squeezed from his being. It seems the trap he had set for me has proven to be his own demise.

You see Chris, I used my skills to augment your formula to levels you never dreamt of; to levels beyond your control.

I lower my head and my voice softens.

I admittedly feel a certain amount of sorrow watching your greatest gift turn into the instrument of your destruction. Your fate will lay heavily on my heart, though by all rights it shouldn't.

I head back toward my car, and I can't help but think about what just transpired.

I did not force him to fight me; I gave him a chance. He forced me into doing what I did, I had to be faithful to my nature.

For after all, I am Gk.

Soon after graduating from the University of Utah, Gk was drafted by a top five-hundred company, if he was to accept the job he would have to move south.

Gk's initial duties were simple enough, to animate local neighborhoods using computer-generated imaging technologies. However, as his duties grew his pay didn't. He quickly realizes he'll never acquire his desired ends by being a servant, even if it is to a major corporation.

So he devises a plan and recruits three others to start a company of their own.

Soon after he was introduced to a woman and it was love at first sight.

He quickly finds his attention divided, but they lived hours apart, and he was able to manage them both. Several months pass and during a holiday party they get engaged. It was truly a joyous occasion, but the hunger for power forever gnawed at his innards and his fiance had dreams of her own.

One of which was to be married shortly after she graduated college, this time quickly approached and when the time came she offered Gk an ultimatum.

Either they get married, or she's moving out west in pursuit of her own dreams.

Gk would soon learn a lesson in love, as well as make his first mistake.

In love, you always follow your heart, but Gk uses his business prowess and lets her go out west.

His reason, he thought she would stay only a few weeks then return. Three years later, he saw her just once.

So Gk and his partners continue on with his company and all seems to be going well.

Their contracts are getting larger and more frequent, at this time he meets another woman.

He remembers the mistakes of the past and vows never to become close to any other woman.

It's funny how things change, when he first met her Gk just enjoyed talking to her and took him several days to remember her name, and his attention was focused strictly on his company. He saw her once every so often and his company was starting to see the ends he desired.

With his recent success, Gk started to make mistakes. He finds himself surrounded by shady business associates, cheap women, and booze.

The woman he had grown to care about, and her him.

They once saw each other every so often, it now became every day and neither of them wanted this.

She once called him her angel, he was now being treated like a devil.

Gk had nowhere to turn, he trusted no one.

Success had the opposite effect from what he expected, Gk saw life as an illusion.

He had friends, but all they wanted was favors.

Buy me this, borrow me that, invest in this, and the woman he had cared about was disgusted by him.

Something had to be done, so Gk does the unexpected.

He sacrifices everything and moves back to his childhood home, this is when his eye's would open.

The mistakes he made would be made no more, for Proud Gk has new goals. His desires have changed, his perception has cleared, and he is now ready to return home. His first goal is to acquire from Joe the device that once belonged to his one-time ally John Walker. With this treasure the doorway to information on every living being can be opened.

Gk wrestled his second away during a rematch he just encountered, this beauty will back the rest of his goals and is the foundation of the dynasty he now envisions. The third Gk acquired from Chris Walters, yet another old friend. This lovely turns out to be capable of manipulating time. Three goals completed, three more need completing. With the completion of all six, what's next? So continues the quest.

Retribution

Dan Phelp, a collector, and that is exactly what he does. He collects strange and rare objects, if it is rare Dan desires it. He has wisdom, knowledge, and skill, but only uses them to gain further rare objects for his already gigantic collection.

Today Dan stands in the study of his treasure house, what else would you call it? His collection could rival even the finest museums, but today his thoughts aren't on his trophies; he awaits a long distance communication, a phone call from me.

Ring, ring.

Yes, in a soft tone Dan answers.

Gk here, I take it you have been expecting my call?

Of course.

Which means you have been monitoring my activities, correct?

Yes, ever since you encountered you rematch.

Then you know what I want?

Yes.

Dan, in the past you and I have had the odd occasion or two to work together; because of this I am inclined to be generous with you.

I fully intend to gain all my desires, but have no wish to cause any harm in the process.

Dan replies, which seems somewhat out of character for you Gk.

I smirk, his reply was somewhat amusing.

I reply, perhaps I'm going soft in my old age.

Dan, as I recall you are known to barter certain items from your collection for even rarer tidbits you crave.

That is so Gk, even though it breaks my heart to part with one of my beauties.

Then you should know Dan that I will soon be coming into possession of something you will most certainly wish to add to your menagerie. Something you would gladly trade, for even the item I crave.

Ah, it would have to be something truly unique for it to take the place of the item you crave Gk.

It is, I shall be getting back to you concerning this matter. Good day, click.

Unless Dan gets back to me first, which means he has unlocked its hidden secret, that he knows how to use its power.

If that be the case, I will have little chance of surviving Dan Phelps response to my offer.

So I wait, sitting patiently by the phone rattling my fingers.

I feel like a schoolboy who has just asked the girl of his dreams out on a first date, I wait.

Patiently I sit by my phone, my patience begins to wear thin.

Nothing! Just as I expected.

Despite his great insight, metaphysics have never been one of Dan's strong suits.

A smile explodes on my face as all goes according to plan. My next stop is to yet another old friend, Scott Stellar. He is a good friend with a former associate of mine who goes by the name Kwik.

I set up a meeting at a local establishment, and pay him a visit. Scott gives me the information on where I should be able to find Kwik, I'm quickly on my way.

My fourth goal is almost within my grasp, or is it?

I'm baffled? This is definitely the area Scott told me Kwik should be found, so where is he?

Standing in the darkness of the emptied warehouse district scratching my head, I hear a loud noise defining to the ear.

In front of me, then behind me, and now headed straight toward me. Ah! It nearly hits me, I barely get out of the way as I fall to the ground, then it stops.

Directly in front of me, I look up and see Kwik sitting on his bike.

With a huge smile on his face he asks, had enough Gk?

I believe I have Kwik, I had no idea your bike was that fast.

Yeah, he says grinning; sometimes it even amazes myself. Confident he continues, and you know why my bikes so fast?

He points to the instrument panel on his bike, it's because of this little darling right here. Adam Perry warned me you'd be coming this way.

You see Gk, I always knew my bike was fast, but I never really knew what speed was until I got this little beauty; in a blink of an eye, he's gone.

Now I sometimes finish races even before I ever realized I've started them, now that's fast.

My bikes quicker than sound, he mentions on his way headed back toward me.

Ha! Ha! Faster than a speeding bullet, my bikes the fastest damn thing on the face of the Earth.

He stops inches from my face as I begin to stand and dust myself off, is it now? Should we test that theory.

Before I can fully stand he begins driving circles around me much like a cowboy circling a calf.

You can hear him hollering, that was a big mistake Gk. Then Kwik disappears into the darkness of the streets, in a blink of an eye, he's gone.

I stand-up, never before have I witnessed such speed and maneuverability, and by what I know of calculating speed and time, it would appear he has nearly doubled his speed as he heads back toward me.

Ah! He nearly hits me as I fall flat on my back.

Face it Gk old boy, there's nothing on Earth that can lay a finger on me.

My bike's just too damn fast, need any further convincing?

No-no! I am a believer, I reply as I crawl to my feet.

With a devilish grin on his face he offers, so here's the deal ol' Gk, we can either do this the easy way or the hard way.

You can either tell me why your so hot to get your hands on all those items, or I can beat you to death at super speeds. With force he repeats, talking or being turned into jelly. Which is it going to be?

With agony I struggle to get up, alright, I'll, I'll tell you everything.

I discovered the true nature of these items while spending time back home, it was a well kept secret for centuries. I believe they come from before recorded times.

They were once a single unit belonging to a lone being, that being built a civilization of limitless power. At that time, they were the only civilization that existed on Earth; they were all that was and all that was, was them.

This civilization lived on for centuries, no one would fault you if you called them Eden. They've been called many names, but I doubt if they had a name or any need for one.

For they were more alone than any has ever been, my voice softens as I continue.

All that was, was already part of them, there was no other in their lives.

I lower my head as I begin to think about what once was, an ache within my heart as I feel a connection, my voice softens even more as I continue.

A more desolate existence is beyond imagination.

I believe that is why they chose to put an end to themselves, but such a powerful civilization does not give up their ghost easily.

From their ashes rose all that currently is, in all its many forms.

I regain my composure; I grow angry and look Kwik in his eyes.

The core of that civilization has separated into the forms of the items I seek, they are the ultimate in power. The biggest secret this world has ever known.

My voice is now filled with conviction.

It was by mere chance I happened upon it while deep in my studies, can you believe it?

The greatest secret of the ages sitting out in plain sight for eons just waiting for someone to discover it.

With such knowledge under my control, I might accomplish my greatest goals.

Kwik stands their with a devilish grin; my, such a touching ambition coming from such a weak man.

Pity, it's a dream that will never be fulfilled.

Hmm, at least not by you Gk.

Ha-ha! The secret of the ages is now mine and mine alone.

My eyes are fixed; I stand-up and my voice is firm.

I think not! I begin my approach.

How did a fool like you ever come to be?

By-by, being the best at what I do, namely racing.

I am also the lone holder of the land speed record.

I stand directly in front of Kwik, well it certainly wasn't for thinking, was it?

The only intelligence you've exhibited so far, is realizing your bike was the only think that could save you from me.

A strategy provided by Adam Perry, no doubt.

We are now face-to-face and I continue, but you still couldn't resist stopping to gloat when you thought I was defeated.

Th-thought, a pathetic attempt by Kwik to interrupt.

My arms crossed I speak with confidence.

Not all weapons are something you would recognize as such, some weapons appear to be nothing more than harmless baubles.

Usually, these are the most dangerous types of weapons.

What Chris had focused time, he was able to tap into it without truly realizing it. It was a subconscious act. Much the way your bike was able to utilize its speed. You made your bike faster, somehow you were able to subconsciously manipulate its speed.

That's why you sometimes finished races before you realized you had ever started, it's called mental acceleration. I start walking back toward Kwik; of course, that's only part of what this wonder can do.

But you're not listening to any of this are you?

You can't hear a word I'm saying, one of the many disadvantages of being fully paralyzed.

I stand with my arms crossed looking down at the once cocky man laying motionless.

You're not so invincible are you? All talk while sitting atop your bike, nothing more.

Though I could leave you like this, you see Kwik I'm not as weak as you thought.

This would be a rough way to learn that fact, wouldn't it?

But don't worry Kwik, I will not leave you in such a sorry predicament, you'll prove more useful to me in a more animated form.

Ha-ha! Tell me Kwik, is this more to your liking?

You know Kwik, when we were kids, you seemed pleasant enough to talk too. A shame you grew up into such a rotter, but maybe you'll learn from this encounter now that I've given you a second chance.

I hook his bike up to my car and Kwik gets in the back.

Don't fret Kwik, we are heading on a little journey, we're going to pay a visit to Dan Phelps.

Dan lives quite a distance away, but I finally arrive outside his treasure house. He has an elaborate security system with heat and infrared sensors, there are also armed guards; much like a preparation for war.

How else would one protect such treasures?

Of course, Dan's ready for me, all set to blow this man to bits the moment I step foot outside his wondrous establishment; so I decide to make my entrance directly through the back.

I find Dan sitting at his display monitor waiting for me to appear, he is terribly surprised as I stand behind him and speak.

You can turn down your defense screen Dan, it is a terrible waste of energy and would not have stopped me had I chose to confront it.

Dan turns and approaches me, so I see.

What have you there?

A prize of great value and extreme rarity; tell me Dan, what would you be willing to trade for such a prize?

Do you not recognize the racer once rode by Kwik?

Dan's eyes grow in disbelief at what he sees unbelievable!

You had best believe it!

A one of a kind bike in mint condition, is it not?

A person could do just about anything they wanted with such a rare vehicle; include adding it to a collection of rare vehicles, like the one you have in this house.

Gk, would you join me in a stroll down the hall that contains my collection?

Most definitely!

I must say Gk, that is a tempting thought.

I would imagine Dan, that owning such a vehicle would make for a crowning touch on such a collection.

We come to a stop.

So which is it going to be Dan, barter or battle?

Hmm, Dan falls silent, but I came here for one reason. Your answer Dan!

Dan raises his hand and offers a stipulation, I will accept your deal Gk under one condition.

Which is? I reply with curiosity.

That a promise of non-interference in my existence accompanies this vehicle.

I smile, as a deal has just been struck.

You have my word on that Dan, and as you know Gk always honors his pledges.

So I've heard, let me have my bike.

You'll find your treasure in yonder display case.

As I'm at the display case removing the treasure I covet so, Dan erupts in hysterical laughter.

It's not a very good deal you've struck today Gk.

I've studied that trinket through every scientific means available, and it is my considered opinion. . .Dan turns to face me.

. . .That it's nothing more than a worthless hunk of polished glass.

With my prize secured I am ready to divulge the secrets this treasure holds.

I'm not surprised to here you say that old friend, to open its hidden secret requires great imagination.

I turn to face Dan, his excitement yields to his curiosity, with my prize in hand I continue.

Something a collector of trivia would be sorely lacking in. the magnitude of this items power is not something you would have accidentally stumbled upon or even easily grasped mentally.

My guess, that more than one mind has been shattered contemplating this trinket. Its potential is beyond the scope of most intellects. With full excitement I revel its secret.

This item can control, reality.

Allow me to demonstrate a mere iota of its might.

The walls become the floor and ceiling, doorways become windows, staircases leading nowhere, nothing is as it seems. I stop, everything is as it was.

With my arms crossed, humbling, isn't it?

Dan Phelps, cowering on the floor barely mutters. I had it in m-my possession this whole time and, t-take it away from here please.

Gladly, I say with pride.

Now only Adam Perry remains to be brought into the fold.

He will not be as easily duped as I was Gk.

I begin to leave, no, I anticipate him being my most difficult adversary. That is why I saved him for last. It is a conflict I must now hasten too, I turn back and face Dan. Before I leave Dan, there is something I should tell you. That bike that belonged to Kwik. . .Kwik enters and grabs Dan.

. . .Has a recovery tracking system attached.

You were going to add my bike to that filthy collection, weren't you?

Dan is truly surprised as he replies, I, I, I .

I bid you both farewell.

Kwik raises his hand ready to strike. You two-bit weaslin garbage-picker, I'll show you!

Before I close the door I turn to face Dan and

Kwik, may all your differences be small ones.

I close the door and am off to accomplish my final objective.

Click.

Adam Perry, the strategist supreme, no longer need he monitor my comings and goings.

He knows fully well where my next destination is, and he's more than ready for me.

He is a champion gamesman, he has spent his lifetime devoted to nothing but the contest.

His nerves are ice, his mind is capable of devising the most complex of strategies, and he has knowledge. Great knowledge all his own, I know he has arranged things so I will have to deal with him on a level of his choosing. After all, he is Adam Perry. Greetings Gk.

Greetings Perry, what will the game be?

Are you not the least bit interested as to why you must match wits with me in order to accomplish your final objective?

I begin to walk toward the gaming table, no!

But I imagine you are going to insist on telling me nonetheless.

Most definitely, to begin with, there awaits the treasure you so covet.

That is a multi-alloy Stoops security system the prize sits in. several layers of shielding protect the item and the base from theft and/or tampering.

I can't help but notice, it appears to be a clear sphere that sits atop a semi-cylindrical titanium base covered by glass, and my prize sits in the center. All I can say is, most impressive.

It gets better Gk. If even one of those layers is breached, the base is programmed to go into immediate operation.

And?

Continuous random destination selection, the item will be instantly transported to an unknown destination.

A destination I will not be able to trace through the base, because?

It will self-destruct as soon as it completes its function, you catch on quick Gk.

And of course you realize, the base is set to activate should anything interrupt my organic vital signs which are being constantly transmitted to it.

Naturally, so in other words, I must play your silly game or forget about ever finishing my objectives.

You'll soon see just how silly this game really is.

The security system is programmed to shut down in the event I lose our little encounter.

What's the contest? Perry.

A quasi-military exercise set on the mental plane of existence. Each contestant will be equipped with an identical suit of body armor. A kill-shot will immobilize the loser and terminate the game program.

I sit down and join Perry across the gaming table.

I take it Gk, you're willing to put up the treasures you have already acquired as a wager in this contest.

Why not? I do not plan on losing.

I have placed my prizes in a stasis field that will deactivate in the event of my death. I always like to play for the highest stakes possible.

We sit there and face each other, much like a test of nerves, and Perry's expression hasn't changed since I arrived.

So Gk, do you have any further questions before we dawn our headsets?

No, it all seems simple enough, childishly simple.

Than shall we begin?

Ready any time you are.

We both dawn our headsets and I must admit, the program is much more sophisticated than I imagined it would be. I could swear the battle armor I wear is real and not some computer-generated illusion, and the gaming arena is equally impressive.

A life-sized chessboard, but with two major differences. The first is that we move on the white squares and the black extend upwards, like giant monuments of different sizes.

And two, we are the only pieces on this virtual field. Like all of Adam Perry's fantasies it has no link with reality, but has a reality all its own.

I also realize in a flash that Perry has lied to me.

I sense the truth of the program, a kill-shot will not just immobilize, it will actually kill.

Kill as truly as if the shot was taken back on the plane of reality, am I surprised? Not at all, I expected no less from Perry. The stakes we play for are astronomical, in his place I would have done the same.

Perry wastes no time with pulmonary jousts, from behind a dark monument he emerges and fires.

He immediately goes for the throat, and I retreat behind a dark square across the way.

I have played this game a thousand times when I was a kid. I know the rules, and how to break them.

And like Perry, I realize the best defense is a strong offense.

I run around the huge square shooting, unfortunately Perry also appreciates the value of a strategic retreat.

Perry comes jumping down from the dark squares, his aerial assault admittedly catches me off guard.

Shots blaze past my head and I return fire to cover my retreat, that was too close.

I move around the dark square and Perry shoots at my reflection in the dark monument.

Before the smoke clears, I sneak into the hole left by Perry's shot.

He follows but doesn't realize, some old tricks are as effective as the first time they were ever used.

Years of experience immediately warn Perry of the mistake he has made, but it is too late for him to do anything about it.

With my arms raised, I am ready to deliver the kill-shot. I can hear Perry say check.

I reply checkmate, a cliche to the end.

Sparks fly, smoke engulfs the arena.

The smoke clears, and Adam Perry emerges.

Ha-ha! I usually loathe cheating an opponent Gk, but the stakes were just too damn high, and you're too dangerous a man to trifle with.

That's why I sabotaged your weapons system before the game, it's a silicon-based fungus you're encased in.

It will permeate your entire being within moments, if it hasn't already.

Ah, ha-ha! You see Gk, I too have begun to realize the true potential of those items, and have desired them myself.

Of course, my studies were nowhere nearly as far as your own but your recent actions confirmed my suspicions concerning them.

So I did nothing to interfere with you taking them.

It saved me the trouble of having to go after them myself, I so hate to travel. . .

At that moment, Perry flicks his finger at what once was Gk, the armor crumbles to the floor.

. . .But I expect I'll find it more tolerable now that I possess all your prizes.

Just then, Adam Perry's eyes grow in disbelief at what he see.

No, it can't be.

Smash!

The computer-generated world Perry's mind is in begins to crumble.

He had figured all the odds, worked out all the angles, thought out every possibility, but in some games, that's just not enough.

Game-masters are not the only ones capable of cheating. Of course, with me already completing the goals I have, I could have beaten Perry in any of a thousand ways, but this method was surely the most enjoyable.

I walk toward the mindless body of Adam Perry and claim my final treasure. He was an idiot for not keeping it on his person, he must surely of known its secret.

It would have told him that it was a double facing him across the gaming table.

For that is this treasures talent, it is a doorway into the mind. But I guess Adam Perry's ego got the best of him when he decided to count solely on his gaming ability, he lived a gamblers life to the last.

I begin to walk back toward my car and I can't help but think.

All-in-all I'm afraid that these people have proven to be a pretty inefficient and a stupid lot, but the glorious ends more than make up for the tedious means it took to acquire them.

Time, heart, knowledge, power, the soul, and reality. So much more than my last venture gave me, all mine. I control it all! I stand there filled with excitement, it all belongs to me!

With time, I can venture back into the primordial past or drive into the far distant future. Time is clay waiting for me to mold it.

With heart, love becomes an intellectual concept.

I consider the possibility and it will be.

With knowledge, no thought shall remain a secret to me. Every mind is mine to open and examine, I can reach out and feel the dreams and aspirations of every human. They touch me, but cannot affect me.

For I am Gk, above such concerns.

My power backs all others, this beauty makes all things possible. I draw strength from the ends, it enables thought to become reality. It is the glue that holds what is in place, it is also the tool that allows me to sculpt in any manner I choose.

With it, I need fear nothing.

The soul, once John Walker used it reluctantly to steal the identities of innocent people, but he was a fool. He had no idea what wonders this tool can accomplish, but I've seen peaceful people turn into a barbaric horde. I've seen sinners turn into saints and saints into monsters.

With reality, how can one explain the inconceivable?

Few rational minds can grasp the myriad activities possible. Scientific laws are within my power to repeal, facts lose their meanings because they no longer have to be. I dream it and it will be.

I return home, my old friend Josh and his wife are there.

Gk stands before you as a force to be reckoned with!

Surely you can sense the changes within me, how could you not? I am power never dreamt of by anyone in the history of this world.

I now am the top rung of the highest ladder, far above everyone else. For they are nothing but part of what I am. All that is will answer to my whims.

I am Gk, I am the head of the table.

Josh has something on his mind, what he is about to say I wasn't prepared for, he has a habit of doing that.

Yes Gk, but sooner or later you will lose it all b y your actions. Do I need remind you of a beautiful woman you once care about?

What?! But she must have comprehended why I did it all. Right or wrong, I did it for her.

I once cared and maybe still do, but I wasn't content on being merely a floor mat for her to walk over. I tried to help in every conceivable way but to no avail, the only interest she had in me was when she needed or wanted something. I never meant to be a threat to her, she was a beautiful woman whom I cared about, I put her above all else.

I lower my head as this is a topic I don't want to discuss, but when my usefulness was over, I found my strings soon cut.

Josh replies, is that what you think?

Then you are a fool, that girl did nothing but care for you.

She didn't come around only looking for favors, when she needed help you were her shoulders. You were the man she looked for, she felt safe in your arms.

For Gods sake, even her son looked to you, but you betrayed them because of your ignorance.

Proud Gk swore he would never again fall in love, but I think you did but wont admit it.

I think she did, but wont admit it.

Well Josh, you seem to be an expert on my life so I'll let you write my autobiography.

Josh walks up to me and places his hand on my shoulder, I'm sure I'm not going to wont to hear this.

Listen Gk, you helped my wife and I when we needed it, I'm just trying to return the favor.

I'm not trying to bring back the past.

You're doing a good job.

Thank you, let me finish.

You were there when she needed you, you tried getting some, but you never forced anything on her. You gave her the respect to let you know when she was ready. Another man would have been gone in days, but not you.

You stood by her, you were a true friend.

I'm sure she seen that, but you didn't and that's why I called you a fool, and now it's too late.

I've heard enough, remove yourself, I'm leaving.

I turn to head out the door, I can hear Joshes wife mention not to do anything I might regret.

The Gk of old would have drunk away his sorrow, but I am a changed man.

I take a walk to the park near my house, there is a bench of to the side. It is a quiet little place off to the side I go to think.

Sort of a rock, a place to be alone.

Was Josh right? I might have care a little bit more for her, but the way it ended, that's not the way I wanted it to be.

I did care for her, but the mistakes that I made. How could I have miscalculated so badly? Gk, the master planner and thinker, I set out on a quest beyond the reach of any but myself. An impossible mission and I succeeded at it, I have wrestled the reigns of power away. No man could ever dream or hope for more than I accomplished. As I sit there my head lowers, I cannot help but to think about what Josh said.

Who could of thought, that my achievements, would prove to be, a hollow victory?

A tear runs down my cheek.

The end begins here

After awhile of thinking about the past, it is time for me to return home, and I know what awaits.

There can be no denying it, you are supreme.

Anything you wish to be, you are.

Anything you wish, is. Nothing in the world would dare challenge that claim, there is only one word to describe you.

As I stand there staring at a picture of the creation of man, Josh continues his ranting.

Within your grasp rests the infinite, my humble personage bows before your grandeur. I am proud to be your first associate and bask in the glory of your presence. What will be my first assignment? Great Gk.

I reply, by falling silent Josh!

The moment is upon us, when the world must come to realize the absolute truth to your words.

I cannot help but think, maybe my goals are set to high. I pound my fist against the wall and watch as the painting I once stared at falls.

I turn to leave the room and comment to my former associate and now current advisor.

None shall deny me my righteous place in the pantheon of this world. I claim my seat, at the head of the table.

On the other side of the country, a man, Steven Shields, a doctor of science who realizes there are secrets hidden within the world that even he, a master of the art of science is not privy too.

Doctor Shields is but a pawn and not some all-knowing being.

At the shields mansion, the doctor is deep within his thoughts. It'd been an uneventful day and my hopes were that the night would be the same.

Alas, such good fortune was not to shine on me.

I was in the midst of a late dinner when I first became aware of the approaching crisis.

Pierce, a servant of Doctor Shields brings a pot of coffee and as he pours a cup he asks, will you be going out tonight master?

Doctor Shields turns the page and replies, only as far as my mind and this book will take me Pierce.

A medical journal master?

It's about an outbreak of insanity in the Catskill mountains.

What caused this epidemic master?

No one seems to. . .crash. . .

By the heavens, what was that?

The loud crashing noise has gotten both their attentions, and Pierce is quick to comment.

Your wife and daughter are out shopping master.

Doctor Shields heads toward the disturbance, hand me my cane Pierce.

It would seem we have an intruder on the premises, one who will surely regret choosing this house to. . .you! I cannot believe my eyes as I recognize the fallen intruder.

Of all the people I imagined might be lurking in my study, Joe was not among the list.

The truth is he wasn't exactly lurking, he seemed barely capable of opening his eyes and moaning.

As Joe lay there, you can barely hear his moans.

Shields. . .must reach Shields.

As a doctor I go to the aid of my fallen friend, you have found me. Pierce, help me get him to the sofa.

We manage to get him to the sofa, and I am deeply concerned about his condition.

Joe, can you hear me?

Barely able to speak, he tries.

Y-yeah, came to tell you.

Tell me, tell me about what?

As I kneel there trying to make sense of the situation, Joe mumbles.

He has them, coming this way, must be stopped.

I'm confused, his words make no sense, who? What?

He has all he needs, Gk is coming!

I know you thought him gone, he was, but is no longer. How could any of us have known, that in his return, he would become all that is.

He feels betrayed, he gave all he could to people, but they took freely and turned when they no longer needed. Such injustice, he thought this an irregularity he sought to right, a tragic mistake he swore never to repeat. So he returned to his childhood home and acquired knowledge beyond that of any living being, through which he would right all the wrongs he caused. Along with his knowledge, Gk has greatly augmented his strength. He would need this might to accomplish the tasks he wished to complete. With concern, Joe continues his explanation to the doctor. Gk now possesses the power to accomplish all he sees fit.

Meanwhile, back at Gk's house.

For long month's Josh I have contemplated the direction in which I should steer my destiny.

All the myriad possibilities, so many choices.

Josh interrupts, I do not envy you, such burdens.

I stand gazing out my window, watching as the sun sets. At times Josh, it seemed I would drown under all the self-questioning, but at long last I realize, there is but one question that needs answering. I am now omnipotent, what should I do with such might? The answer to that, is really quite simple. Anything I want, anything! I am incapable of error, any result that displeases me I can simply reverse.

There is nothing I need worry on, for I am Gk and Gk is boss. Do you understand Josh?

Huh, most definitely, boss.

You see doctor, Joe continues to explain.

Gk lost everything he held dear and he needed to start over, but Gk was too arrogant to be anyone's thrall. His plan was conceived during the few month's he spent back home. That is where he learned of the true nature of the power he sought and he believed his goals could not be achieved without this might. No one realized what limitless might Gk was striving for. Through cunning, sheer strength, and knowledge, Gk wrestled his item's away from those who possessed them. With the acquisition of one, it brought him closer to the goals at hand.

In other words, Gk now has the unbridled power and title of number one. No longer do the laws of nature bind him, his will can bend the very fabric of reality. He is all, and all there is, is now his to command. Gk is now the most powerful man, more powerful than any force. No one can stop him.

Listen to me doctor, such power in Gk's possession is madness. We cannot allow him to hold such rank, we must unite against him, and remove such force.

Pierce, bring Joe a glass of water.

Thank you Pierce, I'm beginning to feel better though I am still having difficulties sitting up.

Please Joe, continue your story.

Alright doctor, Gk returned and sought to find me.

He offered to help build my location, but his motives weren't on business rather on accomplishing His own goals, in which he succeeded.

After which I went to a bar and met up with an old friend, naturally we were tanked. John didn't think so, I tried telling him we should have gotten out of there hours ago.

John replied, I'm getting pretty tired of your nagging Joe.

Hey all I'm saying is, I just lost my location, got yelled at by my boss, and spent the whole night in a bar.

John's blonde-bimbo girlfriend was our driver and she was ready to leave. Of course, she had to add her own two-cents.

Joe, ya just gotta learn to have fun, teehee.

Can't you two get it through your head's?

We gotta find Gk!

John finally agreed and his bimbo took off with the car after dropping us off.

Not realizing the extent of Gk's new might, John and I foolishly confronted him. It almost proved to be a fatal miscalculation on our part.

We were but helpless puppets within his grasp, he toiled with us laughing the whole time.

I thought I was strong, but it was nothing compared to the might Gk brandished.

When he finally tired of us, we managed to flee.

We had passed out for several hours a short distance away. By the time we regained consciousness, Gk had departed to an unknown location.

I believe he has considered the best use he could make of his newfound might. We were informed of this development by his new advisor Josh.

For reasons all his own, he warned that we should unify against Gk, so I immediately set out to spread the word of what Gk has accomplished.

Unfortunately, an event kept me from reaching you until now.

Trying to sit up, Joe places his hand on his head and continues. I just hope I have not come too late.

Hmm, Doctor Shields responds, so do I.

Back at Gk's house, Josh stands there thinking.

I am in awe of Gk's might and his ability to wield it as if it has always been a part of him.

In a thought, Gk and I are off to the location the woman he once cared about works, and at that point I realize his weakness.

Gk approaches her.

My love, I have returned, and it is my most sincere hope that you have at long last, forgiven me for the mistakes I have made.

As I stand behind Gk, it would appear that she hasn't as she turns her back and walks away.

Gk my sympathies, you are not deserving of such brusque treatment.

No, I am not.

Gk watch's as she walks back into her location, and I cannot help but wonder. So much power in the possession of one who has barely reached maturity.

He's only thirty, the very thought boggles the mind.

Gk can destroy anyone he wants with but a thought, yet his basic soul remains entrapped by simple morality. Is he capable of managing the forces now under his command? Or will his fragile heart be his undoing? This fool still pleads.

Listen girl, your scorn wounds me deeply.

It was never my intention to wrong you, you must believe my apology.

True, I did use my resources, but I used them to try and better the environment around you. I sought only to help you, never anymore. You deserve better than this, your best interest was all I thought of.

As she turns away, a friend of hers comes to speak to Gk.

What do you expect? You put her in those situations.

Listen, I know all the stories, a lot of what happened, never did.

You made her promises, and none of which you kept.

I did a lot for her, and asked for nothing.

Look at those two, they're getting heated, and for what? Gk can have any woman, yet he pleads his case for this one.

Look Gk, you haven't learned.

No, you're wrong! I tried my best for her, and she shouldn't have to be bothered by this.

Yes, that's it! What merit has beauty? Be it not respected or honored, how could I gaze so deeply into her eyes and never have realized?

I may now possess ultimate might, but I'm still a man. My adoration for her, was the only trait worth keeping, so fault me not for trying to bring your mind to ease.

As Gk smiles, she turns away from him.

Still she spurns me.

Josh, standing only a few feet away, offers his thought. Perhaps it is because she does not yet realize the true heights your soul is capable of achieving.

What do you mean?

She's been through this before, she is set in her ways. A man must be able to deal with that, are you up to such a challenge?

What?! I turn and face Josh.

Am I not Gk? Do I not hold true to all I say?

I never forced her to do anything, am I not true to myself? So tell me Josh, who under the stars is better suited than I?

No one, but it is not I you need to prove this too.

Yes! That is what must be done. If proof of my change is what is needed, then so be it.

Yet after Gk say's his peace, she turns her back to him. Do not turn your back to me woman.

Her friend interrupts, and adds her opinion.

Gk, she finds your boasts empty, and your bravado distasteful.

You can see the frustration on Gk's face, yet still he pleads.

I do not comprehend this attitude of yours girl.

All I seek is your forgiveness, but all I receive for my efforts is your disdain.

As she walks away from me, I put my head down in sorrow. What have I done to deserve such rejection?

Josh is quick to comment, perhaps it is what you haven't done that riles the maiden.

Of course, so engrossed have I been in reveling in my new found might. That I have been remiss in fulfilling the promises I have made prior.

She needs her own location, so she can further her own goals. It is a promise I made, but have yet to fulfill. How inconsiderate of me, no wonder you have been upset with me. I should always follow through on a vow given.

As I stand there looking at Gk, I can't believe he is really going to do it.

After everything he's been through, out of all the things he is capable of achieving, he is going to help her!

As the doctor stands watching his monitor.

A sense of great unease came upon me, one I could not explain away.

Joe struggles with a headache, as he mentions.

All over the world, I can feel it.

While Pierce begins to shake.

Master, I feel. . .

I shift my attention from Joe, Pierce? What the?

Pierce falls to the floor, and my eyes bulge as I cannot believe what I am seeing.

By the heavens, Pierce!

Joe jumps off the sofa and grabs my arm in desperation. He's dead, they're dying.

Listen to me doctor, if we don't stop him, this business is over. He will control it all.

What are you talking about Joe?

Listen, not one of them knew what happened, it's not going to end.

I grab Joe's arm and attempt to check his pulse, but Joe continues.

I could taste their confusion.

Joe you're shaking, take a deep breath, relax.

It's just too much to bear doctor, too much.

From bad to worse

All is right in the world, for Gk possesses all he needs. The world will now be set right, made over to fit his unique view of what should be.

It would seem as if the whole world is falling into disarray. A jet liner has flown off course and has suffered major damage. It flies in circles as the local authorities try to clear the streets in an attempt at a make shift runway. The panic on the streets is too much to bear, and it appears the media is creating a circus by trying to get the best angles for the story.

With the streets cleared, the jet liner finally runs out of fuel and augur's in onto fifth avenue.

Those passengers were lucky the military was on hand to help out, but they cant be everywhere, and the whole world is currently one big emergency.

As the officers try to remove the doors to the aircraft, words of encouragement are offered.

Just hang in there folks, we're coming!

One cadet will soon learn the true meaning to the word disaster as there is a seriously injured woman in first class. Help me! Somebody please help me!

Oh my, I need assistance in first class!

We'll be there in a minute, one guard mentions as she carries of a child. Its too much Vic, not even the military can handle what's coming down.

We must try Laura, we cannot surrender to despair.

They manage to rescue all one hundred and thirty one passengers without incident, and only a few were seriously injured. Here at channel six we applaud the military and the local authorities on the way they handled this tragedy.

Eric Stoops turns off the television as he cannot bear to listen to the tragedies that are on all major networks.

When the first reports of the great disasters come in, I'll be in my office at Stoops Security Systems wondering what I can do to help.

I figure Max Avery might have some answers, but before I can ask him, over the intercom comes a message. Join us in my office Eric.

Max? Who's in there with you?

One who has made it clear to me just how perilous the worlds current situation is.

And so, the president of the worlds largest securities firm must now undertake a new mission.

Let's go Eric, we've got an important rendezvous to arrange.

Bulletins continue to flood in from all over the world. Disasters mysteriously continue, and half the world desperately seeks out answers.

There can be no doubt what is responsible for this outrage. Yes, these tragedies reek of Middle East treachery.

The President has put America on red alert status, and the powers of the world quickly follow suite.

I thank you all for coming.

I, the President of the United States, would like to call this meeting to order.

My fellow diplomats, as we all know these have truly become desperate times. I must now speak the words I had hoped I would never have too.

Let the war, to end all wars, begin!

The secret room the world leaders have gather in has settled down to an eerie silence.

I am getting ready to sit down for dinner when I am summoned by Gk, without choice I am off.

I've been in many a difficult situation in my life, but I know the very moment I open my eyes, that this is a whole new level of trouble.

I immediately recognize the legendary items Gk owns as the source of his new found might. If that's not bad enough, a few feet away stands Josh, his one time associate.

Yes sir, I'm into it up to my ears this time.

And there is the woman Gk once cared about, a regal sight. I can see why he cares so deeply for her.

As I gaze down the stairs to the main level, it takes me a minute to realize who is stumbling around she's a real mess. It's Gk's cousin Anna.

I'm wondering why Gk has brought me here, I'll soon get my answer as Gk finally speaks.

Tis a family reunion, my dear brother. Let Anna and yourself greet and befriend the woman I care for, Josh is but an advisor.

But Gk, how can this be a family reunion without our father being present?

Father was not invited, nor will he be. Father is a dangerous man, which is why I made sure he doesn't know. He would have tried to abort my vision of the future, I could not allow that.

With a big smile on my face, I reply to Gk.

Then nothing shall, everything is going to work out just the way you want it too, my dear brother.

If there is anything I can do to help?

Gk turns to face me, and shockingly he replies.

Like trying to emotionally manipulate me? What say we see how charming you can be brother while your mouth is tied shut.

Josh takes out a make shift cloth in order to carry out Gk's request.

As my brother turns away, I can hear him mention.

That is how it shall be with all things that irritate proud Gk, annoyances shall simply cease to be.

Back at Shields Mansion, the condition of my unexpected houseguest was such, I thought it prudent to seek outside consultation on the matter.

Fortunately, Doctor Anthony Hill happened to be in town.

Doctor Hill arrives and joins me in my study.

Joe seems to be recuperating just by laying there.

Yes Tony, with his physiology it was the best remedy I could come up with.

Well Steven, it appears to be working.

I must now be going Shields, I need to get to the west coast, with these great disasters going down.

As we walk toward the front door, I'll brief them on what you've told me Steven and you should contact the Pentagon directly.

Of course, good-day Doctor Hill.

Before I can close the door, I am joined by my butler Robert. Master, is something wrong?

Master, speak to me.

Doctor Shields, can. . .you. . .hear. . .me?

Yes, though I've never been contacted quite in this matter, who are you? It would appear the good doctor is in a trance, and is communicating telepathically.

Who are you?

One who may be able to save the world from the disasters, but I cannot do it alone.

The only hope the world has is the banding of all forms of the worlds militaries under one leader.

I must be that leader.

Stranger, I doubt the worlds militaries will blindly follow someone who just popped out of nowhere.

Then your first task Shields is to convince them otherwise.

You are a stranger to me, one I myself see no reason to trust.

There is a method by which that obstacle to progress can be overcome. I can open my mind to you, but in doing so your mind would be bared to me.

It is not an experience I would normally opt for, but the dangers that confront us are too great.

I will take the risk, but be warned though.

If I sense any treachery you shall learn to your dismay why I am called the master of the art of science.

Then Shields, let the melding of minds commence.

I didn't realize, the things you've seen, all so clear to me now.

Enough! Robert tries frantically to awaken his master from the trance he is in. master, with whom do you speak? Master!

Doctor Shields utters, you now have my complete trust, I shall aid you any way I can.

On the other side of the world, it would appear Shields and Hill are not the only two doctors with an interest in the current crisis.

My instruments indicate that the force responsible for the great disasters originated on the other side of the world.

I have never before encountered such powerful readings, yet I'm picking up similar emanations from a small town upstate.

Odder still, these transmissions are be directed to the home of Doctor Steven Shields.

This is a question I must have answered.

After all, this is my world and those are my people dying. No one dares tamper with what belongs to Doctor hector Vance. Plus, there is the fact that great disasters of this magnitude also present a curious intellect with a great opportunity.

A chance to expand on my scientific knowledge and personal power.

At Shields Mansion, they have gathered a few people for the task at hand. This just in, we have an update on the tally of men and women who have fallen in these great disasters. This is bad, real bad.

I can only hope that it doesn't get any worse.

Turn the television off Robert, I've heard enough.

Has anyone contacted Dennis yet? Does anyone know where he's at?

While Dennis has yet to be located, Dennis waits for his boss.

I'm still coolin my heels in this roach motel, waitin for the boss man to make his grand return from the land of sleepin bags. Luckily I finally found a channel on the boob tube that's not obsessed with spendin every second of air time with coverage of the great disasters.

Sittin hear on the floor in my undies watchin an eighties sitcom about a smart mouth lil alien.

Who could of thought cable television being capable of such highbrow entertainment?

I also enjoy the way they deliver beer here, beers always played a big part in my life.

Sure, maybe the rest of the worlds goin down the tube, but as long as I have beer, a good smoke, and some munchies, my worlds okay.

I just opened a fresh beer, and there's a loud crash through the front door.

Unfortunately, the best parties always end to early.

Hey, you made me drop that, and I just opened it.

I gotta hand it to him though, this guy really knows how to make an entrance, a real showstopper.

Well, let me go check things out.

All right mister party pooper, you fixed it so we can't stay here anymore. Where we headed now?

After Gk!

Terrific, just what I wanted to hear.

At the best of times, the resumption of lost consciousness is a jarring, disorienting experience.

At a moment like this however, what?! It can be devastating.

Joe awakes and cannot believe his eye's, Doctor Shields? Doctor Vance? Shields has been detained by two of Doctor Vance's servants. I warn you Vance, you meddle in dangerous matters you do not fully understand.

Then you'll enlighten me, or suffer further discomfort at the hands of my servants.

Joe jumps off the sofa, Vance, unhand my friend or I shall. . .Vance back hands Joe, and he falls back unto the sofa.

You shall fall victim to a superior intellect and strength, as you did last time we meant.

Which is exactly what I did, being weakened from my earlier fight with Gk. I lay there on the couch holding my head, further time is needed for my health to be renewed.

Doctor Vance content with Joe, once again turns his attention to Doctor Shields.

Now Shields, you will brief me on everything you know of the great disasters and the forces behind them. You will speak or I will. . .

There is no need to threaten anyone my good doctor.

It will be my pleasure to tell you everything you wish to know.

Doctor Vance quickly turns around, Joe and Doctor Shields turn their attention as well.

Intruder, who are you?

At one time people called me Michael Gill, you may do so also if you feel so inclined. I believe you know Dennis, he is an ally of sorts.

At Gk's location, you see my dear, the pleasures of having family visit. Amusing, aren't they?

Gk directs the attention of his love to his brother and cousin, as they try to untangle themselves from some ropes they stumbled in.

Josh standing behind Gk, offers his opinion.

It would appear your love doesn't think so Gk.

Eh? Well that situation can be easily remedied, I'll have some entertainment arranged.

Michael Gill continues to explain, and that is how Gk gained his vast might and I came to aid in the thwarting of his plans.

Then you are the man I communicated with earlier, Shields mentions. Doctor Vance, sitting only a few feet away comments on how amazing the story is.

Gill continues, it is a challenge we must meet and triumph over. There is but one way this can be accomplished, I must lead the aligned forces against Gk.

Doctor Vance raises out of his chair, by what right do you claim the mantle of leadership?!

A man who was supposed to have been beaten by Gk nearly a decade ago!

Perhaps, but I alone am familiar with the rank Gk now brandishes, and that knowledge is the worlds only hope.

Doctor Shields raises up and places his hand on the back of Michael Gill. Gill is a man I will gladly stand behind, what about you Joe?

Tis better than following Vance!

With Doctor Vance's back turned, he replies.

Then raise your army and we shall see what comes of it.

Joe stands there looking at the two doctors and Gill, he cannot help but think.

Is Gill truly the best choice? He seems markedly different from the man I met earlier. There is so little anyone really knows about him, how can we be certain?

The entertainment changes and Gk asks, is this improvisation more to your liking my love?

She turns way from the show Gk has arranged.

What? What does it take to earn your forgiveness?

I have given you your every wish and more to boot, yet still you deny me even the slightest of smiles.

I strive only for your affection and approval.

I would do anything to hear you just once speak about me in a positive manner, anything!

Gk pounds his fist on the table and gets up and walks away. From here I can sense the awesome forces exerted by Gk's frustrations. Gk's compassion rises from his location and washes out into the world. He truly does care for her.

On a roof top stands a man, Adam stands on the edge.

I am lost, Mandy is gone. How can I go on?

The truth is, I have no reason too. She and I were linked in so many ways, two halves of a whole.

I am better off dead. I can never. . .what?

At that moment, the building Adam was standing on collapses. The people on the street scatter in all directions, and there is a woman holding her baby.

They are trapped like dears in headlights as a large portion of the building comes crashing down upon them. Logan just happened to be in the area and pushes them to safety. Good God, you saved our lives. That's right lady, but it remains to be seen if I did ya any real favor. As several buildings in the area are now in ruins.

We're flying high above the western coast of the United States trying to get some better readings on certain energy signals. We suspect they have something to do with the great disasters. Suddenly, every gauge on our instrument panel redlines, what?!

The force wave hits us like a runaway train, and it shorts out every circuit in our helicopter.

Gravity kicks in and we begin to fall back to Earth at extraordinary speeds. Fortunately, the Navy has built backup systems that kick-in. That's when we see it. From this altitude it's quite a sight, one that will surely give us nightmares for the rest of our lives. Helplessly we watch as the entire western coast breaks off and falls into the ocean.

We know there is nothing we can do to help, but we have to try. A message from the base comes in Corporal Jennars report. We were coming in for a landing when it hit, there was nothing we could do nothing! There were millions of people in California alone, they're all gone. We just couldn't do nothing. It was, all of a sudden, like the end of the world. Our sensors felt the tremors and traced them across the ocean floor.

Stanley Gault, a member of the Naval Special Forces was deployed to take a closer look. What he discovered was incredible.

He bears witness to volcanic activity creating new landmasses. Not even I, Stanley Gault, one of the most decorated officer of the special forces has ever seen such a magnificent sight. Then my awe is tempered by the realization that the creation of these isles will have cataclysmic results.

There will be tidal waves, probably even now heading toward the eastern coast, deploy a helicopter to search the coast.

Shannon, a naval pilot, it is by sheer chance I'm flying over Atlantic City. It's early morning, and a young couple walks alone on the boardwalk, probably honeymooners.

They hear the roar and look up to see approaching death, they can't move their frozen with terror.

The wave is nearly a quarter mile high, they'll be no escaping it.

The wave comes crashing down destroying the boardwalk and everything else in it's path.

The young lovers are the only two people I managed to save.

Meanwhile, a report comes into the Pentagon.

This is Captain Schmidt calling the Pentagon.

Go ahead captain.

You can inform the colonel that the reports he received about the isles of Japan are confirmed, they are no more. Flying amidst a flock of lost seabirds, it is truly a disturbing sight.

Thank Captain Schmidt for the recon when he returns.

How'd the Pentagon hold up to the quake?

Cracked, but still standing sir.

Thank God! Sir, we're gearing up to be the comcenter for any nation who wishes to help during this crises.

Good move, I'll spread the word. Lieutenant, what about our west coast branch?

I'm accessing them now sir, progress report.

We're setting up house in Vegas, calling in all the reserves.

Same here, we're going to need all the help we can get. Things are getting pretty ugly out there.

Earthquakes, tornados, and floods, disasters have engulfed the Earth, this must be the end.

Back at Shields Mansion, Michael Gill tries to offer a few words of encouragement. It appears everyone fared fairly well thanks to the well built foundation of Shields Mansion.

One of Doctor Vance's servants asks, what was that?

Doctor Vance, never at a loss for words replies obviously an earthquake. Dennis shaking his head comments, sometin must of got God teed off.

Hmm, Michael Gill turns and faces Dennis, he has but only one word to say, exactly.

Preparation for war

Ultimate power at play, an ego gone wild, depraved creativity.

Tell me truly Josh, be it or be it not art most magnificent?

A man and a woman, sculpted out from marble and locked in an immortal embrace.

It is a masterpiece Gk, and a monument to the wonder that is you, but I doubt this opinion be shared by the rest of the world, the creation of this wonder.

Their views matter not to me.

Ah, but I fear Gk, it is a view your love apparently shares.

I look up and stare at her for a few moments, sitting quietly alone, atop the stairs.

What will it take to win her heart?

I turn and leave in sorrow, I repeat, what will it take?

Earthquakes, tidal waves, volcanic eruptions, cities burning. I thought things were as bad as they could get for ol' mother Earth, but I was wrong.

Professor Harding, down in the Pentagon's geosciences lab was the one who laid the bad news on me.

The computers printing its collated analysis professor. My God, it's even worse than I thought.

Professor Harding grabs the report from his assistant and rushes down the main hall toward the colonels office.

Out of my way! Get out of my way!

Colonel! Colonel! I must speak with you immediately!

Later Harding, in case you ain't heard, we got this lil worldwide emergency on our hands!

More of an emergency than even you realize colonel.

You must look at these readouts!

Fine, give me the readouts! These tell me exactly zip! Give it to me in plain English Harding, and make it quick!

Here, I'll lay them out over this table, it will allow me to explain it better. This is a computer analysis of the damage caused by the wave of force.

The one that caused the earthquake?

Yes colonel, but I'm afraid the earthquakes are the least of our problems.

Look here colonel, this confirms that the force wave has derailed our planet from its set orbit.

What?!!

The Earth is slowly drifting away from the sun!

I'm sorry to say colonel, our world is heading for a new, never ending ice age!

Back at Shields Mansion, Joe begins to recovers his health.

The world falls asunder around us, I can no longer put off confronting Gk.

With Doctor Vance, I agree, the time for action is now.

Michael Gill has other idea's though, not yet.

There are forces at work you two do not perceive.

Standing there flipping through a periodical, I weave a delicate strategy which rash actions could rend asunder, patience please.

Doctor Shields steps in an offers his opinion.

We must trust in Gill, I too sense the tremendous forces gathering for a final confrontation.

To strike out prematurely could prove disastrous.

Doctor Vance adds, but the waiting and not knowing what might happen next is maddening.

Gill tosses down the periodical he was reading, then let us be preoccupied with the business at hand.

Doctor Shields, are you prepared to execute the next step in my master plan?

Ready and willing.

Then let us be off.

The two doctors, Michael Gill, and Joe are off, and their servants can only wish them luck.

The situation isn't looking too rosy at the Pentagon. Colonel, we've been having trouble calling in the reserves.

Suddenly, the main doors to the control room opens.

What? I'd seen Doctor Shields do his grand entrance routine before, but what I now find disturbing is the company he is currently keeping.

Who? That man with Doctor Shields appears to be Michael Gill, and that's Doctor Vance with them.

Stay thy hand colonel, Vance is our ally in this struggle.

On this I should take your word Gill?

And the word of Doctor Steven Shields, and the word of Joe.

Joe steps between the colonel and Gill, I know you saw Gill fall in battle against Gk colonel, but...

So then how can he now stand against him on this matter Joe?

Please colonel, Gill replies.

The details of our past encounters are of no importance, all that matters is the mission that brings us here.

Which is?

The raising of an army!

There's mad craziness on the streets, more buildings burning than firefighters and trucks.

A four-story building burns, and the occupants who stand in horror are watching and screaming.

From the crowd you can hear, that firefighters been in there for more than ten minutes!

She's a goner for sure!

My baby! My baby!

The firefighter comes crashing through a second-story window. I'm breathing flames, finding an escape route by sheer luck, at least I saved the child.

She heads toward the crowd and delivers the child to her mother.

Hopefully she'll survive the insanity, more than enough people have died already.

Oh my God! Look, on the fourth-floor!

Help me! For God's sake, somebody help me!

The lone firefighter rushes to help the lady hanging from the window, but it is too late to help.

Before she can reach her, the building collapses.

The firefighter cannot just stand around and watch, when she attempts to rescue the fallen woman debris tumbles on top of her.

Two men standing by rush to her aid.

Ya can't go back in there firefighter lady, she's gone.

Yeah, ya did all you could.

She struggles to talk, but its not enough, its just not enough.

Doctor Shields sends out an urgent message.

I call upon all to aid in the struggle this poor tortured world suffers, your skills and knowledge are gravely needed.

Then Bruce Jennars will just have to answer that call.

You can count Walter Jones in too.

Yet still others join the cause.

Logan, a one-time detective recently laid-off due to his extreme form of serving justice joins the cause.

The dull-witted, yet strong John Brock answers as well.

One-time associate to Gk and traveler, Jacob Harding.

Rodney Thrash, a special forces member.

Stan Gault, another member of the special forces.

The mysterious and formidable Adam Wilson, who recently lost his love joins the cause.

Dusty Coles, a member of the British Brigades.

The beautiful but deadly special forces member, Joan Hawkins.

There seems to be something wrong, Doctor Shields mentions. We have a problem, it seems Richard Blake refuses to join us.

Captain Schmidt comments on how Blake's brute strength would be awfully useful in the upcoming battle. What is his problem?

Bruce Jennars steps forward and answers, he's angry at the military for turning their back on him all those years.

Walter Jones adds, he was one of the founding members of the special forces.

Captain Schmidt replies, and he can be again now that he's reformed.

Then that'll do for now, you can count Blake Richards in, and we can talk particulars later.

And now, the powerful Blake Richards joins the festivities.

Michael Gill makes an announcement, and so our little army is complete.

Richard Blake, cracking his knuckles standing behind Gill asks, so when does this little party get started?

Only when I say so.

Who made blondie the boss around here?

Captain Schmidt steps between Blake and Gill, and replies. Circumstances Blake, circumstances.

Everyone listen up! As you all know we've gathered to take on Gk, and...

Sorry to interrupt you captain, before we go any further I, Doctor Hector Vance, demand to discuss who would best serve as leader of this assault force.

What is there to discuss?

It's obvious that only I have the leadership and ruthlessness suited for that position.

Logan, smoking a cigarette replies, not a chance Vance.

Captain Schmidt steps forward and faces Vance, I thoroughly back Gill on this matter.

From the crowd you can hear, as do I.

Ditto, me too, I think.

Like it or not Vance, we only have one shot at beating Gk, and that's Michael Gill.

Deep, deep, down, you know that.

Walter Jones standing by tries to lighten-up the situation, well that was fun.

The spotlight shifts back to Michael Gill.

Wise decision, you all know nothing of the mysterious workings of the rank Gk now has.

Or the arrangements I made to garner additional allies.

Captain Schmidt asks, what allies?

Powerful allies! Doctor Shields, Joe, are you ready?

As ready as we can be.

Then captain, I leave you in charge until my return.

Let us be gone Joe.

Where did they take off too?

To an unknown location.

Outside the disasters continue, but Marc Allen, a firefighter just doesn't believe it.

He stands on a rooftop near a major bridge.

My guess is that an oil refinery upriver ruptured during the quake and something ignited the escaping gas and oil.

We stopped a merciless gang from torching the city, but now it's burning anyways, and there is nothing I can do to stop it.

The fire will take out half of what's left of the city. When will it end? And what will be left when it does?

Sitting at a window, in front of a full moon, Adam speaks to his friend. To tell you the truth Walter I'm not sure I'm up for this.

These are some of the toughest people gathered here.

Don't waste your time worrying about it Adam.

They all put their uniforms on the same way you do, one leg at a time.

You wouldn't have been called up if they didn't think you could cut it, you'll do just fine.

As I walk away, I can't help but think that I just wish I were as confident as I sound.

Face it Jones, we're about to take on the most powerful man in the whole dang world.

Odds are against any of us living to see tomorrow.

Erik stoops and Max Avery have arrived at the destination, at a classified location they await the arrival of their invited guests.

When's this summit going to happen Max?

Soon Erik, soon. Now?

Michael Gill and Joe?

Welcome, Gill turns to Max and questions, they have not arrived yet?

The gathering has been awaiting your arrival.

None of my experiences have prepared me for anything like this. I know whom they are from stories told to me, but to actually be in their collective presence is overwhelming.

They are the leaders of Earths special forces.

Frank Bradley, the head of Earths security patrol.

Reporter to the world, Sean Stevens.

Yet another high member of Earths security patrol, Jake Roberts.

Ed Ortiz and Jose Garcia, the Earths balance.

Morgan Phillips, the worlds judge of only the most pressing issues.

The powerful master of arms, Duncan Simon.

Directors of Earths forces and master philosophers, Jena Yates and Dale Howard.

The hunter of treason, the powerful Norman Brooks.

And those two in the corner can only be diplomats.

With an overwhelming look Joe mentions, I was expecting neither Frank Bradley or Morgan Phillips.

Gill replies, their presence also comes as a surprise to me.

Before Gill can get this summit going, a strange turn of events.

I, Frank Bradley am the actuality Gk strives to take over. I come seeking judgment from the one man I consider an equal.

And so, Morgan Phillips stands present at Frank Bradley's request to hear his case.

Please Frank Bradley, state your case.

Gk seeks to unbalance that which is, to throw the nature of this world into a maniacal entropy.

After hearing Frank Bradley's comments, Morgan Phillips takes a moment and replies.

I have considered the matter and cannot concur.

Gk only strives to replace your importance in the world with his own.

Natural selection is one of the worlds oldest cannons; the strong replace the weak.

It is as it should be, no crime is being committed.

Morgan Phillips shall not become involved in this matter.

Morgan Phillips turns and leaves the room they have gathered.

Shortly following, Frank Bradley leaves as well.

Erik Stoops confused asks, Frank Bradley's taking a powder, why?

Michael Gill once again ready to get this summit underway replies, perhaps he has his own agendas to pursue. It matters not, we will deal with the forces still available to us.

Yet another surprise as Sean states, whose numbers I cannot be counted among Michael Gill.

I remain here only to observe and record the events that are ahead of us, I will not take up arms against Gk.

How sad, I had hoped that the current crisis would allow you to put aside that resolve.

I know Gk has been more than kind with you.

Nonetheless, I believe the powers gathered here are more than sufficient to execute my plan of attack.

Michael Gill will soon learn though, that this legendary grouping is not easily influenced, as Norman Brooks stands before him.

Your plan of attack?

You expect Norman Brooks to follow one such as you into battle?

Gill answers, that is why I am here.

Norman Brooks does not heed the empty words of insects, especially one such as you!

Then Norman Brooks is a fool.

Joe standing next to Gill realizes his friends mistake, as he tries too. . .Norman, no!

With such raw force, Norman Brooks attacks Michael Gill as retribution for his insults.

The force exerted knocks Joe back as he cannot believe the fate laid down upon Michael Gill.

Norman Brooks now takes control over this summit.

We face a dire peril my fellow diplomats, our defense will be more easily planned without yammering weaklings to distract us.

Does Norman Brooks always let his anger so badly cloud his judgment?

Who?

Just a yammering weakling who knows that naked power is seldom the answer to any problem.

Surely you must realize that even this groups combined might is nothing compared to the force Gk wields. Only a richly complex and skillfully executed strategy will insure your survival.

Time is short, and I have such a plan.

Norman Brooks, we know this Michael Gill, he is capable of wondrous deeds. Ed Ortiz and Jose Garcia have weighed the options, and choose to join forces with Michael Gill.

Soon the rest of this legendary brigade follow suite.

Max Avery and Erik Stoops also ally themselves with Michael Gill.

As does Duncan Simon and Jena Yates, Dale Howard, and the diplomats apparently.

You can include Jake Roberts also, Gill.

Michael Gill turns his attention, what now proud and mighty Norman Brooks?

Hmm!

Back at the Pentagon, Jennifer Starling sits there thinking.

Never before have I felt things so tense around the Pentagon before, the waiting's got me going up the wall. As she tries to gain insight on the current crisis, she asks Chris Redding.

Red's, what do you figure our chances are of beating this Gk character?

Next to zero.

Huh? But didn't we take this dude down a couple of times?

Not exactly, in instances we won the day, but not without help.

You mean from Erik Stoops and Michael Gill?

No, I mean from Gk himself. In both instances Gk provided us with the means to thwart his plans.

Whether he did so consciously or subconsciously, I do not know.

Then you're saying?

That our fighting forces can defeat Gk, only if he wishes to be defeated.

And if he doesn't feel like getting his butt kick?

Then everything we are trying to accomplish, is over.

I know what you are!

Red's, what was that?

Something we best look into Jen.

Such a gathering of might will always hold conflicts, in the other room a conversation between Bruce Jennars and Doctor Vance becomes heated.

You're a vicious, cold-blooded snake who does not care for anyone but himself! You see this crisis as just another opportunity for better solidifying your own stature! You're planning on grabbing whatever you can out of this mess and the blazes with the rest of us.

That is my way.

Why you!

Captain Schmidt grabs Jennars from behind, alright Bruce, cut it out.

While Chris Redding subdues Doctor Vance, taking advantage of our hospitality is inadvisable doctor.

Captain Roscoe confronts Jennars, Bruce, you're out of line. Captain Schmidt, take Bruce in the other room to cool off.

And as for you Vance, I begin to wonder if the dissension your presence creates doesn't negate your usefulness.

The upcoming battle will make that determination, captain.

Michael Gill and Erik Stoops enter, and Gill questions, what transpires here?

Captain Roscoe answers, just a minor domestic dispute.

Wasted energy, better saved for dealing with Gk.

And when can we expect this battle to begin?

Within minutes, my impatient captain. I've only a few last minute details to attend to.

Where can I find the former detective Logan?

From the gathered crowd someone answers, I saw him heading toward the roof.

Captain Roscoe responds, what? Blake Richards is up there.

From the crowd you here, those two have tangled more times then I can remember.

I better. . .no captain.

Allow me to handle the situation.

Alright Gill, just remember those two don't see eye-to-eye.

Back at Gk's location, Josh asks Gk, how long has he been there?

Only a few minutes, but Sean Stevens' coming heralds the beginning of hostilities. Fools taking up arms against omnipotence. They rush head on into Armageddon, it shall prove to be a most glorious battle. Surely the heavens will run red with blood, but in the end, as always, Gk shall stand triumphant.

On the roof of the Pentagon sits Richard Blake, he sits on the edge thinking.

I couldn't take being cooped up with those jerks anymore. Huh?

Just wanted some air, didn't mean to disturb you.

Ya couldn't stick around either, huh?

Logan lights up a cigarette and joins Richard Blake on the ledge.

Logan, I didn't expect you to be like those other wimps.

How come?

You and I have had some down and dirty scraps, you fight someone, you get to know them really well.

And?

And, I've come to the conclusion that I like ya shorty.

Why's that?

Because in our own ways, we're both the same pal.

They turn their attention behind them as Michael Gill begins to speak.

Which is why I wish to speak with the two of you alone.

What's on your mind fancy pants?

Life and death. In a short while, we confront Gk, a man with unimaginable power whose sole goal is not yet known.

Your point?

Extreme measures may be called for in dealing with him.

Meaning what?

You and Richard Blake have an outlook on death the others do not share, except for Doctor Vance, but he cannot be trusted.

In other words, if we get the chance. You want us to sanction Gk.

Michael Gill turns, that is as good a way of putting it as any. You're a bit of monster yourself, aren't ya blondie? We are what circumstances make of us, and heads back down stairs. It begins to snow and Logan's quick to comment. Snow, in May?

At Gk's location, he stands before the woman he so cares for.

They have gathered together and come to confront me.

My love, will you stand by my side?

As she has before, every time Gk asks her a favor, she turns and walks away.

It is as I expected. I deluded myself into thinking you could ever care for me, but one such as I has no need to suffer a void of affection. Gk shall not stand alone, all things are possible for Gk.

My love, meet Kellie Baker, she is everything my soul longs for, Kellie is everything you are not.

Standing before Gk, such a vision of loveliness.

Long flowing blonde hair, an hourglass shape that could rival even the finest models. Sophisticated and kind, her touch is warm and her devotion is to me. She is the balm to soothe the ache within my heart, I no longer have any need of you.

While Kellie falls into Gk's arms, he watches as the woman he strove only to make happy walks away.

Kellie begins kissing him, and you can see a gleam in Gk's eyes as he watches her walk away for the last time. A tear runs down his cheek.

This is not the time to let his emotions get the best of him. There are other, more important matters ahead of him, and Gk is more than ready.

Let the warfare begin, let the blood and entrails of my opponents scrub away my pain and sorrows.

Call to arms

At the Pentagon, Michael Gill gathers his troops.

Defenders, the time is upon us.

Prepare thyself for a battle most fierce and awesome. Doctor Shields will instruct as well as transport you to the precise location each of you must be once the battle commences.

Each of you has been briefed on the line of attack you should institute. The lives of your fellow combatants depend on your following this plan. Doctor Shields will remain behind to monitor and apprise me of the situation from each of your points of views. He will also facilitate the evacuation of any combatant too injured to continue the struggle.

I wish…

…wish each of you, the best of luck.

Let us be away Joe.

Where are we going?

Little ways away from Gk's current position.

He should be at his location, can you see him with those far-ranging binoculars?

Yes, he's looking our way.

I do not like being held in reserves Gill!

My health has returned, I should be part of the upcoming battle.

And you will be Joe, but only when the moment is right.

But our allies will need my skills during the initial assault.

Joe, you still do not comprehend our situation, do you?

Perhaps not, there appears to be much you have hesitated in sharing with your comrades.

Joe, let me explain in ways that will make it clear to you. Gk's might is unquestionable!

The aspects in which he controls are inconceivable!

He quite literally commands all there is, he is invincible, utterly omnipotent! These statements are not grandiose rhetoric, they are the truth!

Back at the Pentagon, heads up everybody.

Time to get this party started.

On your mark, get ready, get set, go!

Joe, our allies combined might is less than nothing against Gk's might.

They stand defeated before the battle has even begun. The true purpose of their attack, is merely diversionary. They are sacrificial lambs, and may the heavens forgive me. This is exactly as I planned.

The allied forces reach Gk's location with each setting up in their instructed location.

Captain Schmidt begins the assault.

Follow me, we must be merciless if we are to have any hope of victory.

My brother Gk is insane. He beholds four of the mightiest fighters, with Captain Schmidt leading the assault. Along with Bruce Jennars, Jacob Harding, and Stan Gault all pouncing to the attack, and what does he do? He smiles, but maybe he has good reason too. After all, strength is one thing Gk has in abundance. The ability to halt the incoming onslaught is just one skill Gk has mastery over.

It appears this conflict will not live up to expectations, and will not be much of a battle after all. Of course, Gk has sparred his entourage the indignity of such fate.

Josh, the woman he strove so hard to please, our cousin Anna, his new fling Kellie, and of course myself. Even the enigmatic Sean Stevens was sparred, what use is omnipotence if you have no audience to flaunt it before?

Gk approaches the combatants as they stand motionless, are these the best they could send against me? Such a puny force, with but a thought I could terminate their annoying existence.

Josh, always willing to seize an opportunity brings to Gk's attention.

There are two others you might wish to include in your thoughts Gk.

The one you acquired your first item from, Joe, and my one-time comrade Michael Gill, returned to once again plaque me.

They seem to be the only two people in the world intelligent enough not to challenge my omnipotence. Still, they should be dispatched with the rest.

Gk, stay thy hand. The unseemly interruption may be opportunity disguised.

Speak your mind Josh.

You have power without limit, yet still you fail to win the heart of the lady you care so much for.

These buffoons may prove useful in changing that.

How so?

Courage Gk, all female hearts, even one so cold toward you is warmed by the sight of raw courage.

Courage, such as exhibited in battle. Yet such bravery only exists when one faces the prospect of death. Meeting that standard would require balancing the terms of battle so that these fools actually stood a chance for victory, something not beyond your ability to arrange.

Yes! Yes, yes I can do it. I need only cut myself off from all sensory input. I would retain limitless might, yet not know my opponents next move. That would allow them less than one percent chance for victory. Not the greatest odds in the world, but perhaps good enough to impress her.

Watching Josh and my brother, I can't help but think. What game is Josh playing?

It was most subtly done, but Josh has just saved the lives of the men and women who have gathered against Gk, and engineered the possibility of Gk's death.

Josh has used deceit to play upon the confusion my brother is experiencing adjusting to his newly elevated state of being. It seems the forces against Gk have a most unlikely comrade.

Who? I sense someone behind me. Oh, it's just our cousin Anna. In an attempt to win back the woman he cares for, Gk divulges his plan to her.

Prepare to witness warfare never before seen under the stars my love. My diminished capacity now turns this conflict into a true test of nerves and battle skills.

Josh and my brother prepare to resume the conflict as they walk away and head toward the combatants.

A masterful plan Gk, I do believe I saw a gleam in her eyes.

Then let that gleam be fanned into a roaring flame, let the battle begin!

The opponents sent to defeat Gk, have fallen to the floor with bone-jarring results.

Ah, ha, ha, ha, ha.

My brother just stands there laughing. Then, the unbelievable occurs.

The dull-witted John, and the incredibly strong Blake Richards take Gk by surprise.

They unleash massive punches and Gk falls back into a wall. He truly has dampened his senses, love truly has befuddled his reason. Gk is actually playing by the rules, how out of character.

These two behemoths are quickly on top of him, pummeling my brother into the ground.

Yet, do even these mighty fighters stand a chance against Gk's vast might? I doubt it.

They are but bothersome fleas to my brother, and Gk throws John much the way a child throws a rag doll.

Blake Richards notices this and starts to land some huge punches. So this is the hotshot who wanted to lay challenge to us? Landing punch after punch.

He doesn't look like much to me. You can feel the force exerted by Blake Richards as he pounds Gk into the floor. This creep isn't even trying to defend himself, easiest battle I. . .I. . .ever. . .what?

How? Gk stands up with a huge smile and takes a powerful swing of his own, and Blake Richards can only retreat. With Gk's attention directed at the fleeing Richards, he is unaware of Chris Redding standing behind him.

Though their cause is hopeless, I must hand it to them. Their battle strategy is first-rate and flawlessly executed. A lesser man would surely fall before their assault, but not Gk.

Chris Redding begins to attack my brother, but he is no match as Gk grabs Chris and throws him into a wall. Chris will soon learn defeat as Gk approaches, but just before he's on top of Redding, my brother stops.

Gk comments, amazing! I would have never expected such an avenue of attack. Of course, it's Captain Roscoe who leads this fighting force.

It looks like we have Gk confused! Pour on the power! Follow the plan, and hopefully a few of us might survive!

Jennifer Starling and Stan Gault begin their assault on Gk. Their combined punches back Gk up, but it is in vain hope. I can already sense my brother adjusting to his situation and taking control of this battle.

While these two punch mercilessly in hopes to prevail, Michael Gill and Joe remain a small distance away.

How goes the battle Joe?

As expected, I should be with my friends fighting by their sides.

That would be utter folly Joe.

And why is that?

Because you have a major role to play in this little game.

Which is?

All in due time Joe, what you don't know, Gk wont stumble upon.

Doesn't that same risk exist with him reading your mind?

No! Gk knows me, he will not risk such a distraction while in the midst of battle. Gk has narrowed the scope of his might, just as he was beginning to adjust to it. His mind must be reeling from the changes. Of course, that makes him no less dangerous.

Gk backhands his merciless attackers, away from me you clowns!

Stan, Stan! There is something growing where Gk touched us.

It appears to be some kind of moss, remove it quickly.

Sorry Stan, my brother would never lay a trap so easily evaded. The moss has now permeated their entire beings, and to their sorrows there are truths that cannot be denied.

He is Gk, and his name means triumph.

The old campaigner in Gk begins to return, this type of battle has always been his forte. Any hopes I foolishly held of the combatants triumphing over my brother quickly fade. Yet hope never dies, Captain Schmidt swings an iron club and knocks Gk to the ground.

Hope is a universal condition within humans, unfortunately treachery also resides in some hearts.

Doctor Vance seizes this opportunity, that power, I must have Gk's power. And by doing so, he denies Captain Schmidt a second blow with his club.

Doctor Vance, back off! You're in the way!

That rank, it will be mine!

Such greed always creates its own reward.

A trap set by Gk blows the crooked doctor nearly thirty feet. Doctor Vance tastes the bitter nectar of Gk's wrath. Fortunately, Doctor Vance's defense system saves him from suffering total defeat and destruction. But once again, a valuable lesson goes unappreciated. Vance lands after bouncing nearly thirty feet, and still larceny is his only goal.

I will not be denied that rank!

Captain Schmidt throws his club at Gk while he was distracted. One who has always known such truths, fights on despite all odds.

And in turn discovers new, more horrifying realities.

Gk, as if he had seen it coming, blocks the deadly projectile.

Such a move takes the captain by surprise, and he is forced into hand-to-hand combat.

Have to make every punch count. So savage is the captains attack, that even mighty Gk is momentarily taken back. Sadly, spirit will only take one so far in an encounter such as this.

Gk grabs hold of the captain. Power is the only capitol honored in this high stakes game.

He throws Captain Schmidt like a child's toy.

Captain Schmidt was the highest card in our hand.

Gk turns his attention as yet another combatant begins to attack.

'Tis Jacob Harding, yet another fool rushing to defeat.

Whose strength will put an end to this madness Gk.

Highly unlikely my boastful friend!

As Gk pounds Harding into the ground, the unexpected happens, the miraculous. He is the former detective Logan. Of all the combatants, he would have been the least expected of delivering the deathblow.

Logan jumps down and buries two daggers in the chest of Gk. Gk looks Logan in his eyes, and then my hopes plummet from the mountain heights to the depths of the darkest valleys. Gk breaks his wrists, and the most vicious of the combatants flops to the floor helpless.

Vance, you return for another shot at my rank?

Only death will stay thy hand GK!

That can be arranged!

Meanwhile, Michael Gill and Joe are paid an unexpected visit by a powerful ally.

We grow restless and wish to join the battle.

Not yet! Now be gone before Gk senses your presence.

Gill! That is mighty Frank Bradley you speak too.

Just another piece on the game board as far as I'm concerned.

That's all this truly is to you, isn't it? A game!

If I allow it to be any more than that, I could not go on.

Unable to speak, Gk's brother continues to bear witness to the defeat of this army. They are falling like dominos.

My heart is deeply touched by the valor I witness here today. The might Joan Hawking and Dusty Coles wield is nothing compared to Gk's might.

They know this, yet still they press the attack.

Dusty Coles grabs Gk from behind, and Joan Hawking employs her martial arts.

Gk turns his attention first to the lovely Joan Hawking. My brother has always been kind to women, so he removes her from this battle.

He now turns his attention to Dusty Coles.

I avert my eyes, as I have no wish to remember such horrors.

A masterful move, Dusty Coles steps back when least expected. My brother pitches forward, off-balance and the special forces member Bruce Jennars moves in for the kill. Unfortunately, the agent's power is not equal to his battle prowess, and now Josh joins the fight. Gk allows him to vent his anger and frustrations on the decorated officer.

My brother once again sets his sight on Dusty Coles.

He places him in a chokehold, cutting off oxygen to the combatant. He struggles only for a few seconds, then Gk throws him to the ground.

Captain Roscoe rushes to the aid of his fallen friends, while a once successful ploy is tried again.

Chris Redding sneaks behind my brother in hopes of catching him off guard, but Gk never falls for the same trick twice.

He catches Chris and grabs him by the throat, Gk delivers a punch of such force that Chris falls immediately.

And yet another valiant effort fails.

He's dead! Captain Roscoe yells as he rushes to his fallen comrade. You murdered him! You cold-hearted monster!

My, such an emotional outburst, not at all what I would have expected from the legendary Captain Roscoe.

Unless it serves to create a clever diversion.

Adam, once thought to end his own life when he found out his beloved had passed, now may play the most important part in this battle.

He grabs Gk from behind in hopes of detaining him until back-up arrives.

You did it Adam, but can you hold him?

Don't know captain, I think I. . .No!

Gk breaks free and grabs Adam by his throat.

He slams him into the ground, I cannot be detained!

I am absolute!

Captain Roscoe, trying to buy some time replies to the Man-God.

You are not capable of holding such rank, you will eventually fall, or be toppled.

Jacob Harding wraps a rope around Gk's neck, while John begins to assault my brother.

Ah, ha, ha, ha, ha.

Gk laughs at their defiance, and I am chilled to the soul. For there are truths in the Man-Gods howl.

I look around and see the woman Gk cares so much about. She knows this, I can see it in her eyes.

She has no doubt of this conflicts outcome.

No battle is this, just slaughter to feed an already oversized ego. The only person not fascinated by this outrage is our cousin Anna.

Poor Anna, for her shattered mind and body are beyond all caring. For her broken psyche leaves her on the brink of oblivion, she would be far better of dead.

Still, some dreams refuse to die. Some souls never no when the cause is lost, such ignorance can be truly awe inspiring.

Gk disposes of mighty Jacob Harding and the dull-witted John, they are lost to this world.

Gk, my love, I have discarded of those that have been a nuisance to you.

My thanks Kellie, you prove to be exactly what I had hoped for. A woman who shares the same values I do, a woman I might even come to lov. . .what?

Walter Jones swings into action, drop-kicking Gk.

He's all yours Captain Schmidt, I'll take care of the bimbo.

Now your in for it Gk, Captain Schmidt takes a huge uppercut swing with an iron club. Gk goes down and Captain Schmidt continues his assault.

You've destroyed half of this army Gk, your time is up.

Captain Schmidt raises his club high above his head, it is now time to pay the piper!

That's it captain! Stay not your hand! My brother must die, or all is lost!

Good God! Gk has paralyzed the captain!

A grim, bottomless acceptance of our fate finally claims me. Gk is inevitable! He is invincible!

All that is left are tears, and the echoes of dreams shattered.

Rodney Thrash tries his hand at Gk, but his efforts may be too late.

Back off old man! No ones gonna finish off Captain Schmidt while Rodney Thrash is around!

Not round, square. Square as in cubes. Like a child's toy blocks, Gk disposes of Rodney Thrash and finishes off Captain Schmidt.

Turn and face me Gk.

Finally the reserves are called in.

You are Erik Stoops, the late Edgar Browns replacement, and head of the worlds largest securities firm.

It shall prove your downfall Gk.

Erik throws a quick left/right combo, but Gk catches both and snaps his wrists.

You suffer Stoops, suffer from unwarranted delusions of grandeur.

My brother finishes the job, and Erik Stoops will suffer no more.

I look around and see the fallen combatants who fought a valiant fight.

Captain Roscoe, the man in charge of this fighting force approaches my brother.

It's not over until the fat lady sings Gk.

Surely you jest.

Never been any good at stand-up routines.

Or at organizing an assault I see.

We tried.

This is the moment Michael Gill was waiting for.

Joe, ready yourself.

Now?

On my call.

Captain Roscoe approaches proud Gk.

As long as one man stands against you, you'll never be able to claim victory.

Noble sentiments, from one who is about to die.

Gill, now! Gk is going to kill him.

Wait, Joe, wait!

Gk, I lived my life by those sentiments, there well worth dying for.

That's close enough captain.

Huh? Captain Roscoe looks down to see his feet bound to the floor.

Gk replies to the captain, then die you shall.

Gk is always pleased to honor such a foolish request.

Gk raises his hand in order to deliver a crushing blow.

At that moment, Michael Gill yells, now!

Joe is off, racing toward Gk.

Michael Gill watches, Captain Roscoe stands his ground. Gk's hand is at the peak of its might, and Joe rushes to complete his task. Joe misses his mark, and Gk retains his rank.

The echoes of failed plans and good intentions, wasted in futile acts. Nothing remains as hope, nothing remains but sweet oblivion and an end to this nightmare.

Captain Roscoe makes an attempt by punching Gk across his jaw. Like a bothersome flea, Gk smacks him.

My brother looks around, what have I been doing? Must have been out of my mind! They came so close, I nearly lost it all. Let me once again be all that I can be, I will myself back to full strength.

I wish this battlefield cleared of all remnants of the folly I nearly allowed. For I sense a far greater struggle about to begin.

Joe returns to the side of Michael Gill and offers his condolences.

It is as I expected Joe, we tried to do this the easy way and failed. Now begins the conflict I strove to avoid. It may well prove to be a battle the world cannot survive. Frank Bradley, it is now your turn.

The world leaders stand to confront Gk, and despite my best efforts, I cannot shut my eyes to the awesome sight no man was ever meant to see.

Armageddon commences in but seconds, and I have a front row seat for the event. I pray my end comes quickly, for the world is about to become a place I no longer wish to be a part of.

My name is Sean Stevens, my sworn task is to observe and chronicle great events that occur in the world.

My curse is to always witness, and never participate. I must be true to this duty, even on the brink of Armageddon. A contingent of Earths highest officials challenge Gk's might. Such a conflict may well prove more than our fragile world can bear.

Gk, we call upon you to surrender your rank. Honor this request, or face power beyond your wildest dreams.

Gk replies, I believe you will discover the horizons of my imagining far wider than you would suspect. You address omnipotence, tread carefully.

Armageddon

That which you seek to challenge Ortiz, is beyond even your vast intellect. Be gone fools, or suffer my wrath.

While Gk awaits a response from those who would dare challenge him. Josh comes by and offers a few words of insight.

I believe your brother is about to put on quite a show for us. With such forces aligned against him, Gk will surely unleash the full fury of his might.

Still the outcome of this battle yet remains uncertain. There will be no time to worry about or energy to be wasted on nonessential priorities.

Such as this location or relatives, I doubt you'll last more than a few micro-seconds into the conflict. It should be a quick death, and of course, Gk has the ability to rebuild his location afterwards. He'll make it as good as new, unfortunately you wont be around to see it.

Meanwhile, Doctor Shields calls Gill to find out their current situation.

It is inevitable Gill, Earth is falling into another ice-age. What transpires on your front?

The army I built has fallen and been exiled, please try your best Doctor Shields to locate as many as you can for later retrieval.

Meanwhile, the leaders of the world have engaged Gk.

Doctor Shields cannot believe what he has heard.

By the Holy Ghost, an engagement of that magnitude could...

Sean Stevens bears witness to the engagement and in his own words.

The forces unleashed in the initial clash are beyond the power of words to describe.

Many of the edicts of nature fall victim to the assault. I sense near collapse along the entire spectrum, fear grows within my heart. The fear that I am witnessing the end of the world.

The effects a this confrontation ravage entire buildings in the immediate vicinity. Calculating the lives lost as a result of this confrontation will have to wait, but even in the midst of such destruction I am awe struck by the mysteries of the soul. Gk's brother felt certain that death was near to claiming him, the only thing greater than his surprise at finding himself among the living. Is discovering who his savior is, the woman Gk only tried to make happy. Her hatred for Gk must reach unfathomable depths. At an unknown location Michael Gill and Joe confront their nightmares.

Gill, I had no idea it would be so!

Yes, sheer luck we survived, too close.

Gill, what's going on?

That building, it begins to crumble. Quickly, we must be away from here, if we do not get away in time, we will be lost!

A perilous world, where each second reveals a new and greater danger. Case in point, Earth jarred loose from its orbit and drifting away from the sun.

It is about to have a new doom visited upon it.

Its woes increase a thousand fold as snow begins to blanket the Earth. The remaining inhabitants begin to loot and pillage what remains of the emerald jewel. Yet such worries seem hardly worth mentioning when considered in context.

For our world wait's a mere breathe away from all encompassing destruction. A doom birth and nurtured within the dark ambitions of those jealous of Gk's might. Gk defends his rank, let the world tremble.

The two diplomats draft countless soldiers in to the conflict, using them as weapons of war.

They march helplessly following orders, the fact that some of these soldiers have families cannot be a consideration in this globally spanning contest.

With the speed of thought, their menacing potential is neutralized by power without limit.

But a second later it becomes apparent, that their sacrifice was but a ploy, a diversionary tactic.

For the true thrust of the assault comes from Jake Roberts, who seeks to bury Gk deep within the wells of his mind. A futile hope, for one of Gk's abilities gives him mastery over that which seeks to overwhelm him. It be like trying to drown an ocean, and Gk disposes of Jake Roberts.

Yet defeat is answered by renewed vigor. A two-front assault by Ed Ortiz and Jose Garcia. They hope to dichotomize Gk, a divide man is an easier man to deal with. However, Gk refuses to surrender his individuality and disposes of the threat.

The battle continues to rage without pause. Forces combined to add up too more than the sums of their totals. The temporal is abandoned for pure force.

The sheer intensity of Norman Brooks, Max Avery, and Duncan Simon's blitzkrieg catches Gk off balance.

Yet it is but a minor setback for Gk, one that can be over come with but a mere wish.

This is utter folly Gill! Those seeking to defend it, are destroying the world. Such insanity cannot be allowed to continue!

And how do you plan on stopping it?

By love, as Gk will soon learn.

By the heavens, what am I doing?

Giving those wretches exactly what they deserve!

But they are my brothers, my equals.

And I shall destroy them all!

No, I should honor and cherish them.

What madness is this!?!

Conflicting emotions, tearing me apart.

This can only be the works of, Jena Yates and Dale Howard. How dare you tamper with me so?

Be gone bothersome manipulators!
But Gk must also beware of deceivers.
What the Hell?
Exactly Gk!
Josh?
Come to relieve you of your burden of supremacy!

A responsibility I am not yet ready to relinquish traitor! Aacck! Gk grabs this traitor by his throat.

You revert to type prematurely Josh, a mistake you will pay for dearly!

A that moment, before Gk can finish Josh, a blinding light knocks him to the floor.

What? Who?? You too betray me?

The woman Gk only tried to make happy stands between him and Josh.

I offered you the world, I gave to you freely.

You and your sons happiness was my only concern, but you let those bothersome insects spread lies about me. They filled your head with delusional thoughts and instead of talking to me you. . .NO!!!

The woman he loved, steps aside and the full force of this legendary brigade showers down upon Gk while he was distracted by his emotions. And she can only watch as the man who would love her most is brought to his knees.

But Gk is power incarnate, he quickly regains his composure and succeeds at his mission.

'Tis truly best this way.

Supremacy calls form clear thinking, unburdened by chaotic emotions. Let me be rid of all illusions for I am Gk, I am supreme.

Who is there to argue with Gk's sentiments?

Joe and Gill have taken notice that the worldly disruption has abutted.

The war continues Joe, do not delude yourself into thinking otherwise.

That crumbled building, I had friends that lived there. There might be some still alive amidst the wreckage, we must search them out.

I would advise against it Joe.

I believe I had more than enough of your advice Gill.

As you wish, it's just a heart, even one as strong as Gk's, can only take so much.

This berserk conflict must end Gill.

Not until Gk is stopped.

Why are you so hard pressed against Gk?

For reasons all my own, but know this, unless his reign topples, this fate awaits the entire world.

After imprisoning the world leaders, and sending his beloved home, Gk looks up to see the true reason he's here. I have been expecting you.

Now that his foot soldiers have fallen, proud Frank Bradley at last deigns to show himself.

To reclaim that which is mine and myself, control of all that is.

A prize I fought hard to gain, and one I shall never abandoned.

Then Gk, let us see which almighty power truly has the tighter grip on the fabric of what is, defend yourself Gk.

In a blinding light, the two powers confront each other. Surely this must be the end!

No! the outcome of yonder battle has already been decided Joe.

How can you know this Gill?

I am linked to Gk in ways even I don't fully understand, the mastery of all actuality is now firmly in the grasp of one individual.

Gk or Bradley, who prevailed?

One who only losses when his subconscious desires betray him.

You mean?

I do! And in that slim hope does survival lay.

More riddles Gill? Is speaking plainly beyond your ability?

Perhaps Joe. Doctor Shields, retrieval is in order.

Joe, we must be off.

Where too?

Back to Shields Mansion.

Doctor Shields asks, how goes the struggle?

It appears Michael Gill and Joe have conflicting views. Michael Gill answers the doctor's question, poorly. While Joe answers the same question, horrendously.

The nature of energy is to dispense.

The nature of despots is to contain, conflicting tendencies. By the heavens, Gk has succeeded in imprisoning even all-powerful Frank Bradley, all is lost. Gk sits motionless in his chair, the battle surely took a lot out of him.

Gk, my lover! Speak to me!

And what would you have me say dear Kellie?

Gk has now thoroughly taken control as he claims Frank Bradley's rightful place in the pantheon of this world.

I, Sean Stevens, can only conclude, that a valiant effort to stop Gk, has failed.

Gk, your body?

No longer needed Kellie. Magnificent Gk has rid himself of the flesh. I have shed all vulnerability!

As he did once before, when he gained all his desires. Then as now, Gk underestimated the strength of will. Especially will sparred on by hatred, deep within Anna, vengeance stirs.

Gk's own cousin, Anna snatches away the rank he fought so hard to gain.

Nooo!

A senses shattering return to flesh.

My love. . .I could not reach her in time. . .

I. . . A reversal of dire fortunes.

Raising her hand in triumph, Anna steps away from the edge of oblivion. The mantle of providence now rests on new shoulders.

My every wish is but an urge away, and you know what I yearn for dear Gk? Revenge!

How the tides have turned, Anna disposes of Gk and Kellie.

Back at Shields Mansion, Michael Gill senses what just transpired.

The reigns of power have switched hands.

How?

Our situation has gone from bad to worse! The newly christened almighty is deranged from months of pain and anguish. Shields, I will need your talents.

Trapped and alone! For I had not the foresight, and Kellie was not capable of surviving such force without the aid of my now forfeited rank.

Gk holds the lifeless body in his arms, I shall miss you. Survival be not a treasured prize, my body shall endure, long after my spirit succumbs to this punishment the fates have chosen for me.

A lifetime of emptiness, a lifetime to mull on my losses and follies.

What? Who?

Welcome to Shields Mansion, Gk.

Why have you brought me here?

Yes Gill, why did you bring him to my home?

So I might destroy you Gk!

Joe, no!

He does not hear my warnings, and now Gk and Joe battle viciously in the living room.

Back Shields, neither of us has the ability to separate these lunatics, but you can call on those who do.

Way ahead of you Gill. I was only able to locate these five before your return.

They will do nicely. Gentlemen, if you'd be so kind.

Blake Richards and Captain Schmidt detain Gk, while Jacob Harding and John hold off Joe.

Doctor Vance remains behind me, I still believe personal gains are his only want, but I don't have time to waste as there are other, more important issues ahead of us.

Now, if you two are quite through, you might be interested in how we might save this world from destruction.

Which is exactly where it is headed, with my cousin in charge. Her intellect is not up to such control!

Sudden omnipotence would be a crushing load for even the finest minds, for Anna's scared psyche, it must be overwhelming.

Total confusion rains as she strives to adjust to the deluge of universal sensory input.

Suffering the nightmare of abruptly becoming aware of all life and matters. Most certainly the thought of escaping into catatonic oblivion enters her soul.

Pray that she does not surrender to the urge, for the entire world would join her in that dark journey.

Then it is agreed, we go with my design.

Captain Schmidt stands and replies to Michael Gill.

Your plan stinks of risk, but I see no alternative.

Nor do I, Shields adds.

In that case, a word alone with Gk is needed before we can proceed.

Doctor Vance is quick to comment, so you can scheme up some new deviltry against us?

I tell you this Michael Gill is obviously Gk's secret partner.

The others leave and Captain Schmidt must coax Vance out.

To the door Vance.

You fools, you will regret not heading my warnings.

They use to be comrades!

They're all gone, well comrade, what now?

Straightforward conversation.

You know we need your help to overcome your cousin.

And what if I withhold this aid? What benefit do I reap from her defeat?

The truth!

What truth?

About yourself!

Let me guess Gill, you have some special insight into the matter.

Yes! I was part of your rank, while you possessed it. I know you as no other in the world does, better than even you know yourself.

Look back onto your life, Proud Gk, and what do you see? You see a man always seeking ultimate power and losing it as soon as he attains it, and why?

Because deep in his soul, he cares too deeply for the people around him.

Three times you have triumphed over incredible odds to gain the ends you desire, and three times you have subconsciously supplied the means to your own defeat.

You let Anna rest the rank you fought so hard to gain from you. Just as you allowed that fool, who in his wildest dreams couldn't amount to half of you.

Convince the woman you tried so hard to please, to turn against you.

No! it was a mistake!

Even I, err. . .

I didn't. . .I. . .I. . .

I will aid you, but afterwards, no promises.

None expected. Let us join our allies in the other room Gk. Doctor Shields, is all in readiness?

Everyone's set to go.

They begin to leave, and I wish Captain Schmidt who is leading this force to fight well.

We shall give it our all Gill.

Michael Gill, Doctor Shields, Joe, and myself stay behind to go over some last minute details.

They haven't got one chance in a million for victory Gill.

But we do Gk.

Yes, one in a million.

At the location Gk built, Anna and Gk's brother are standing there, and she turns to reveal what she has learned.

Already the mist begins to part. The future clears for me, and so does my destiny. I begin to understand Gk's hunger for this might. Tomorrow is mine to sculpt to my fancy, the world is clay waiting to be molded. Never again will I be victimized or surprised. For I have seen my every waking moment, stretching off into forever.

In fact, a most satisfy moment is almost upon us.

In exactly five seconds form now, I will be receiving visitors.

Finale

Two old foes, and three others whose recent actions have earned them my animosity.

Doctor Vance, Blake Richards, John, Jacob Harding, and leading, Captain Schmidt. They strike as one.

Their combined might could easily rend asunder a small army, but against Anna and her new might, they are nothing.

She easily imprisons them and realizes that this is merely a momentary diversion. They are but children sent to pester, a means to attract her attention.

The architects of this fruitless assault are now noticed and tracked down by my limitless senses.

You'll find this interesting my dear cousin.

There are three who wish to challenge my might, and one of them is. . .they turn to greet their visitors.

. . .Your brother, Gk!

I've come to reclaim my rightful property, wench!

With the help of your two little friends? You disappoint me Gk! I thought you'd make your last stand armed with more than just empty bravado.

Power! It is a quality that must be cultivated and nurtured. It is a reward to be earned through intellect and patience. It cannot be gained and held through chance, in the wrong hands, it will only prove, self-destructive.

At a location a small distance from the Drive, Gk approaches his cousin.

And so you see dear Anna, even though you have usurped that which is rightfully mine, it shall do you little good. Return my property immediately, and all shall be forgiven. I might even appoint you my chief consort, if you behave yourself.

Joe, standing only a few feet away from Gk is confused. Anna said "two little friends", but three of us accompany Gk?

Anna replies to her cousins offer, a very tempting offer Gk. Hmm, but, she imprisons Gk.

I take this to mean, that my kind offer has been rejected.

As ever Gk, your keen intellect amazes me, right as usual.

Anna is unaware of Michael Gill standing behind her.

Doctor Shields notices this and comments to Joe.

He stands outside the usual realm, and Anna cannot sense him.

Gk sees this as well, that his cousin is unaware of Gill's presence. He begins to smile.

I see no good reason you might have for smiling, old man.

Which clearly illustrates the pathetic limits of your own intellectual capacity. You haven't the vision necessary to properly wield such rank.

Oh, but Gk, I suppose you do!

Just look at what I have accomplished so far.

Great deeds, such as destroy half the world!

They challenged me, lets just say, thinning out the herd.

It was sheer insanity Gk, you couldn't even keep a blindly devoted woman close to you.

It just proves dear Anna, it was a grandeur beyond your comprehension.

Sophistry! Your reign as supreme could not be allowed to stand, and by my newly acquired power, I shall see that it does not!

Michael Gill motions to Doctor Shields so he can take action, as Gill can sense what is about to unfold.

Anna takes center stage and decrees.

With the exception of my rank, let everything be as it was, twenty-four hours ago!

No! Gk cannot believe what he has just heard.

The wish becomes reality, half the world is resurrected mere moments after its unexpected death.

Most will remember nothing of what has occurred.

Some will have a nagging feeling that something is, or was amiss. While others will remember, but that memory will prove maddening.

For it will function just how truly helpless they are. Powerless, against a force beyond their comprehension. A will capable of either causing genocide, or returning a frozen planet to its proper orbit. So let there be celebration through out the world, for Gk has fallen. The reigns of supremacy once again shift hands, but for better or worse? The game continues.

Behold, a new day dawning. For a mere wish gave birth to the world, for my dear cousin Anna willed that everything be as it was. I am free.

I walk over to my fallen cousin, and offer to point out the mistake she has made.

You see Anna, when one has such power, she should be very careful what she wishes for. Wishes, are sometimes fulfilled.

I now reclaim, what is rightfully mine.

Before Gk can reclaim his rank, Anna reanimates herself.

A mistake even the wretched thing that I was, can rectify with but a thought. While your error Gk, was gloating, when you should have been grasping the power you crave, will not be so easily remedied.

Ah, touche!

With Anna distracted by Gk's imprisonment, she is unaware of Michael Gill standing directly behind her.

What? An attempt by Gill to snatch the reigns of power away from Anna, fails.

How? How is it that you two still remain?

Of course, the Doctor! Well we'll brook no further mischief from you.

Gk's quick to comment, another error in judgment Anna.

But one again I promptly righted Gk!

You have been truly fortunate so far, but as you are about to learn, some mistakes are worse than others.

When you least expect them, they return to haunt you.

With a freighting feeling, Anna turns around.

The leaders of the world!

Gill, why are we back at Shields Mansion?

Because Joe, it is all part of the plan.

What?

The threat to the world could not be neutralized until the rank of power was in other hands.

Because Gk would have sensed it and stopped you?

Yes! Anna's inexperience and current confusion is our only edge.

From the beginning, you knew Gk would lose control of such might.

Because I know Gk, and the way his mind works.

So what now Gill?

I do what must be done, but I will need your assistance.

In what fashion?

Joe, can you not guess?

Back at Gk's location, the world leaders have learen't well from our initial encounter.

They attack now en masse, rather than diffusing their might in individual efforts.

My cousin Anna's bewilderment with omnipotence, and her light grasp on her newfound might, must surely be sensed by them.

Their strategy is obviously to hammer her with an unrelenting assault, thus keeping her from concentrating on a multi-level plane of existence.

So her full strength is not allowed to be brought into play. As expected, my cousin doesn't see this, and has fallen victim to their ploy.

Of course, such a tactic would have proven futile against me.

Back at Shields Mansion, Gill has informed Joe of the plan at hand.

Joe, you now know all that is Michael Gill. The scope and particulars of my plans are now clear to you?

Yes, but illumination and understanding are not one and the same.

Gill, I cannot fathom your attitude toward this entire situation, toward all life in general, so detached.

Emotional nerves cauterized I suppose, but some how I manage. It is of no importance at the moment, once again the world needs saving. It all sounds rather mundane when said like that, doesn't it Joe?

that's what men like you and I do, even Gk, when he's not bent on the pursuit of supremacy.

But there is a battle going on, and it was only a matter of time before Anna got the upper hand.

She possesses power without limit, with such might any dullard would eventually prove victorious.

Now everything depends on Michael Gills timing, it must be perfect, or all is lost.

Joe looks around, Gill, where are you? Gill!

Nowhere, everywhere, at one with the world!

From one, I reach out to all!

Anna, triumphant over the world leaders, stands and proclaims that a new order exists within the world.

All hail the coming of omnipotent Anna!

Gk, bear witness to the birth of a dynasty which will last many a millennium, perhaps forever!

What do you say to that?

Let there be, disharmony!

A blinding light, aargh! What. . .is. . .this?

Retribution, my dear cousin!

For Michael Gill was successful at separating power supreme from Anna. Gk breaks free from his imprisonment.

My dear cousin Anna, you learen't that ultimate power proves to be a mantle not easily worn.

Now observe how such rank should be properly wielded. Gk reaches down to reclaim his rank, but before he can do so. The five sent to distract Anna, now find themselves trying to stop Gk.

Stay thy hand Gk! Quickly my friends, such rank cannot fall back into Gk's possession.

However, with such might up for grabs, no one is trying to stop Gk. They all want it for themselves, as they all rush to claim it.

Mine! You idiot, I'm on your side!

As they all wrestled to claim the greatest prize in the world, it has become every man for himself.

With only one prize available, only one can claim ultimate supremacy.

Let the conflict end!

Looks like there's a new supreme being in the neighborhood.

And Michael Gill's first move is to free and send home the world leaders. And I will deal with all matters in my own fashion.

Gk steps to the forefront, that rank belongs to me!

You would only lose it again Gk, you really don't desire it.

Anna steps forward to mention, are you fools going to let him grab such rank? What right has he to it?

I have the right of possession, that is enough.

The power supreme is now Michael Gill's, seek not to dispute that claim. I promise to use it wisely.

But what about these two? Gk is mine!

Blake Richards and John approach Gk in an attempt at detaining him.

Unhand me you dull-witted brutes.

Gk backhands them, and they both fall to the floor.

I suggest you puny fools put some distance between yourselves and my person.

What?

A thermal detonation device on my person, set to detonate in fifteen seconds. Click.

Why?

Because, I would prefer death, to living with the guilt of failure. Pride, my one fatal flaw.

Captain Schmidt rushes to the forefront. There's no time to deactivate the bomb, everybody stand back!

The captain hits Gk with such force, that Gk launches out into the streets.

The force in which he hits. . .BOOM. . .

A spectacular explosion, what a way to go.

Exactly what I would have expected from my brother.

Gk is no more, this madness is over, we leave you Michael Gill.

So be it.

What? The others are gone, yet still we remain, why?

Because, Doctor Shields, Captain Schmidt, and of course, you Joe. Have each gazed into the depths of my heart.

Before you came power incarnate.

It makes no difference Joe, my soul is known to you three. Go fourth and tell the masses, that Michael Gill is a man who can be trusted.

We're not so sure we can truthfully do that.

You aligned an army against Gk so you can claim his rank, and the fact that power corrupts is a truism that cannot be ignored.

You fear my rule?

Surely you must realize, that even before Gk you lived under such fears.

But it was a benign fear, random and uncalculating.

Now that it is calculated, you find this unsettling?

Afraid replacing your usual existence of uncertainties with order might prove unpalatable?

Already the distance between what I was and am is insurmountable. Like an ant, contemplating the cosmos. I knew it would be so, yet still I hoped.

I guess there is really nothing left to say Joe, good-day.

I go visit my associate Dennis.

What's happenin Gill?

We are heading on a little trip.

Where too?

I begin a journey mapped out amidst the stars, 'tis a path I cannot stray from.

Nice place it's led ya to so far, where the heck are we?
An out of the way location, through that wild brush.

Impossible?
That word no longer holds any meaning for me Dennis.
So what are we doin here?
Paying a visit?
On who? And why?
Why? Because it is what I always do after gaining such prizes.
Always?
Time is a repeating loop to me now.
Look! The wild brush clears, and in the field, Gk?
Merely an empty shell of what was Dennis.
A scarecrow?
Behind the stuffed model, Dennis notices.
That house, you've got to be kidding?
There is no humor in reality Dennis, greetings Gk.
I should of known I couldn't fool you.
As you know, the world no longer holds any secrets from me.

The memory is dim Gill, why have you waited so long to gain vengeance?

Must you always ask the same questions Gk?
I suppose so, confusing isn't it?
I seek not revenge Gk, advice is what I crave.
Endure, or surrender the rank.
Puny words of comfort, aren't they Gk?
As you well knew they would be.
Tell me Gill, where does supremacy go from here?

To a confrontation, to a resolution, and then on to yet another confrontation. Time has taught you the folly of such an existence, has it not Gk?

Three failures of such magnitude, are enough, even for me. A quiet life will allow me to digest and incorporate the lessons the past has forced upon me.

Then I wish you luck Gk, farewell.
We walk away, but Dennis is confused.
Gill, you're not plannin on leavin Gk runnin free, are you?

Merely apiece, like all others, that is the mosaic that is now my world. Without Gk, the picture is incomplete.

Well, if you say so.

Power, such an ephemeral commodity.

Hard to gain, easy to lose, and I thought I once understood it, what vanity.

I take a seat on my front steps, and I can't help but think. Michael Gill, a man who wished nothing more than to spend the rest of his days within a peaceful and quiet environment. He now possesses power supreme, and all the responsibilities that goes with it.

While I, whose entire life was dedicated to the pursuit of supreme power, now find myself living in a quiet environment. Left alone to think about where I went wrong. Irony worthy of a drama.

Yet strangely enough though, I envy not Michael Gill. For somehow I feel, that in the long run, Gk has come out ahead in this particular deal.

The End

Portfolio

simpler times

nature's glory

About the Author

Giorgio will arguably be considered one of the most inspired writers of all-time, and one of the most potent forces in this new era. He has many traits which include among others architecture and design, but he exerts his greatest influences through his writing. Giorgio was born in Chicago and his attachment to his hometown and its culture is apparent in his works. He spent his late-teens and early adulthood in Utah attending their University where he was brought under the training of some of the greatest designers in the nation. Giorgio is neither easy to get along with, nor easy to understand at times, but he is able to put emotions on paper, feelings that can't be expressed with words. In short, Giorgio is more than a man, he is divinity. His personal life thus far has been a litany of failed relationships and misdeeds, yet his works are able to capture the imagination of every genre. Giorgio is a unique individual with the highest levels of compassion and an intellect that is unmatched. He is a man that takes great pride in his works and after reading his books or meeting the man, you will walk away with a rejuvenated outlook on life.

Printed in the United States
54929LVS00004B/14

9 781418 469429